A Very Corporate Affair

Book Two

D A Latham

DEDICATION

To my dearest, darling Allan

ACKNOWLEDGMENTS

With thanks to all my advisors

Thomas Darlington

Andrea Mills

Michael Harte

Rebecca Elliot

Johanna Ballard

Penny Harrison

Gail Hayward

and

Trystan Lutey

CONTENTS

ISBN-10:149059910X
ISBN-13:978-1490599106

CHAPTER 1

Once again I sat in the ante-room to Ms Pearson's office to find out what my future held. I felt the familiar fear that the meeting would be to tell me I didn't fit into the ancient, top law firm, even though I'd been assured by my manager it would be to discuss a promotion and pay rise following my coup at gaining Retinski Industries as a client for our firm, and the influx of other blue chip clients which had followed Retinski's lead. It was only three months since I'd finished my traineeship, and been given the opportunity to join Pearson Hardwick's corporate division. I knew that promotions and pay rises generally took years of hard work, and it could be argued that I simply got lucky, because the owner of Retinski fancied me. The truth was that I had worked my butt off on his account, and had delivered the goods, efficiently and within the time allocated. I had also headed a team of fifteen lawyers and five secretaries, which had also gone to plan.

I had a good fallback position, as the day before, a Sunday, I'd had a phone call from a head-hunter working for a rival law firm, sounding me out as to whether or not I could be persuaded to move. The figures discussed were tempting, but I was happy at

Pearson Hardwick, and felt a sense of loyalty towards the company which had given me my big break into corporate law. It didn't hurt to have a backup plan though.

I tried to calm myself. Mrs Pearson was the managing partner, and was a super-sharp woman who didn't miss a trick. I didn't want to show any nerves, or self doubt in front of her. *I should be confident about this*, I told myself. Retinski, Ivan Porenski's company, was likely to net Pearson Hardwick at least two and a half million a year in revenue, with five other large, blue chip companies following Ivan's lead, and instructing us as their legal representatives. With an extra ten million in revenue predicted that year, I should have been swaggering around, instead I was sitting worrying about getting demoted to the back room for not being 'posh' enough. It was an inbuilt inadequacy that I carried around, the feeling of being an outsider. I didn't attend the same schools as my peers, and had clawed my way up from the council estate. I covered up my humble start in life by being dedicated, focused and hardworking. The strategy had seemed to work alright so far.

Ms Pearson's secretary interrupted my musings, and indicated that I should go in. I knocked on the door first, and on hearing a cheery 'come in', opened the door. Ms Pearson was sat behind a large, pale oak desk. She gestured to the seat opposite, and after shaking her hand, I sat down. She peered at me through her stylish little glasses.

"Elle, how lovely to see you again. It only seems like yesterday that I was sending you over to corporate. Yet you appear to have made quite an impact."

"It's been a busy time over there, but it's an enjoyable busy," I replied, trying to gauge her expression.

"You appear to be quite the star of the show Elle. I gather from Mr Carey that you have made quite a mark. It's very impressive. Now, I asked to see you today for two reasons. As you no doubt know, we don't normally review pay or position until you have been in a role for a year, but Mr Carey is concerned that you may be approached by our rivals due to your coup with Retinski. Can I ask if that's happened yet?"

"I've been approached, yes."

"I see. Can I ask what your response was?"

"I listened to what they had to say. I didn't give a response. I have a sense of loyalty to this company, and I would prefer to remain working here, if that's at all possible."

"What did they offer you?"

"I'd rather not divulge that information. I'd prefer to listen to what you would like to offer. It makes it fairer." I looked her straight in the eye. Keeping away from a Dutch auction would earn me points for integrity. "I'm projected to be gaining the company approximately ten million pounds worth of revenue this year, and six blue chip clients. I'd like you to bear that in mind."

"Of course. What kind of ball park figure do you have in mind?"

I took a deep breath. "Around 250 thousand per year, plus a bonus structure that is based on what I deliver."

"I see. That's a very big ask for someone just out of a traineeship."

"Yes, I know, however I have billed nearly three hundred thousand this month alone, plus delivered six new clients. I'm aware that my work output rate is extremely high, and I have contributed to the impeccable reputation of the firm by delivering a difficult project quickly and efficiently, plus giving added value to the client." I was talking about a project I'd done for Ivan's company, uncovering a massive fraud as well as setting up a new payroll and HR system, which had been flawless.

"Now, as I said, there were two reasons to speak to you today. We have also been approached by Lord Golding, chairman of Goldings Bank. He has sounded us out about handling some of the bank's corporate work, the areas that the regulators would prefer to see the transparency of a separate company, rather than the bank's in house legal team, so our area would cover corporate governance, and overseeing the auditors. He requested you as his point of contact as well. My concern is that seven clients would be too much for you. How do you feel about that?"

"If I'm being paid well to do it, I'm happy to take on a challenge." *Damn Oscar, what's he playing at? Doesn't he realise an ex is an ex?* "Plus, the backup I've received from my colleagues has been first class. It's a great team at corporate."

"Good. I like your attitude Elle. I think in light of Goldings coming on board, 250 thousand a year is probably not unreasonable. I hope that outbids our competitors?"

I nodded, "and the bonus structure?"

"A standard 10% of revenue. I can also move you on to the grade one benefit package. How do you feel about that offer? What I can't do at this stage is offer you partner status, I think it requires more time and track record."

"I understand that Ms Pearson, and to be honest, it's not something I would expect or demand at my stage of career." She nodded. "I'd like to accept your offer, and go and crack on with my work if that's ok."

She smiled widely. "Good negotiating Elle, I think you've been watching Lewis. I'll communicate the new package to HR and let you get on." We shook hands, and I left. I wanted to punch the air in triumph as soon as I was outside, and it took every bit of willpower I possessed to remain calm. *I'm on a quarter of a million a year!!! Yipidee do dah!!* I screamed inside. I popped upstairs to see Lucy while I was there, for a five minute catch up over a cup of tea. She was doing well in the family law department, and we agreed to meet up again soon.

As I headed back to Canary Wharf, the only other person I text with the good news was James. I knew he'd be asleep as California was nine or ten hours behind, but he got up early, so I figured that I wouldn't have to wait too long for a reply.

I had missed him that weekend. Although we were only flatmates, we'd become great friends, and shared a lot of the same interests and tastes. The flat had seemed a bit quiet and lonely, and apart from a couple of yoga classes, and a visit to the supermarket, I'd barely seen a living soul. I'd ended up working, which was a bit tragic, but clearing up my paperwork meant that I could hit the ground running on Monday morning.

Back at the office, Lewis pounced as soon as I walked in. I followed him into his office, and we sat down to discuss the week ahead over a coffee. "Did you ask for what I told you to?" He asked, fixing me with his sharp stare.

"Sure did. Managed to get a good deal. Thanks for guiding me on that," I replied, unsure if discussing salary was a good idea.

"Good. Glad to have been able to help." He trailed off, clearly wanting to know, but not wanting to ask me outright. I changed the subject instead.

"Did you know Oscar Golding has retained us for his corporate governance work?"

"Yes, I heard this morning. Another coup there Elle. It's a lot for you to take on though. I think I may have to assign you a small team. Laura has a list of the companies who have requested you as their contact, so I suggest that you set up meetings with all of them, get to know them, and find out what they need. Don't forget to inform them of all the extra services we can offer that they may not know about, or considered using."

"Will do. Do we have a resident expert on bank auditing?"

"Carey. He knows all there is to know. He can assist you with that one. Now, I took the liberty of arranging a company credit card, as I expect you to entertain some of these clients, dinner, that kind of thing. It's being delivered to your office today. Easier to organise expenses."

"Ok. I've done the expense forms for last week, and the invoices to Mr Porenski's firm. They've already been emailed over to accounts, along with the time sheets, and other paperwork."

"Good. I'll let you get on."

I drained my coffee, and made my way to my own office. Laura was at her desk working at her computer.

"Morning Elle, got your schedule for this week. I emailed it to you. I also emailed you a list of people you need to call and arrange meetings with. The phone's been going mental this morning."

"Thanks Laura, and thanks for all your help last week. We really nailed it." I went and settled myself in my office, and switched on my computer. I groaned when I saw my schedule. I had lunch meetings almost every day, plus two dinners arranged with clients, plus I still had a list of new clients to make contact with. Pearson Hardwick were definitely going to get their money's worth out of me. I made a start on my calls. Ivan had recommended me to several company CEOs, who were keen to meet up. By the time I got to the end of the list, my schedule was terrifying. The last name for me to call was Oscar. I took a deep breath before dialling his number.

"Lord Golding's office" said a bright, cheery, voice. I explained who I was, and was connected right away.

"Elle, thank you for calling."

"You're welcome Lord Golding. I understand you want Pearson Hardwick to take over the governance work for the bank?"

"I do indeed. You don't need to be formal with me Elle, please call me Oscar. Yes, we've been using Odey and Corbett, but in light of the high praise your firm's receiving from all sides, I thought it was time for a change. I hope you don't mind me requesting you as my contact, only I know how exact and precise you are."

"That's fine Oscar, I don't bear any grudge. I'm delighted to welcome you as a client. Just let me know how Pearson Hardwick can assist you." I kept my voice even and professional. I was determined not to allow Oscar to rattle me.

"Would you prefer to discuss this in either of our offices, or would it be better to meet for lunch?" Oscar was testing me. I didn't fancy going to his office just yet, not with the memories of what we did there last time so fresh in my mind.

"I have a mad schedule this week, all the lunchtimes are booked for meetings already. I can do Wednesday afternoon at three in my office, or tomorrow evening for dinner?" I cringed slightly as I said it, but part of my job was to wine and dine clients, and Oscar was now an important client. *Sly bastard,* I thought.

"Tomorrow evening would be great. Should I book somewhere?"

"That would be fine. I'll pick you up around 7.30?" I was determined to maintain an element of control.

"Oh, ok, sure. I'll see you tomorrow." He sounded puzzled. Truth was that I didn't want him anywhere near my flat. Tomorrow night he'd be meeting 'Professional Elle', not his ex girlfriend, 'compliant Elle.' I added it into my already mad schedule, wondering when I'd get time to do the mundane chores that keep my polished persona alive, and looking respectable.

My phone chirped with a text from James.

well done little Elle, kick ass ms lawyer. Pleased 4 u. Wish I was home 4 celebration

I met the first of my new clients for lunch that day, the CEO of a major software company, whose firm were considering a flotation on the AIM market. I took him to lunch in the Italian restaurant on the ground floor that Oscar had introduced me to.

His name was Steve Robbins. He was in his late forties, rather geeky, and extremely nervy. He explained that he had begun his company in his spare bedroom many years ago, and had grown it himself to be a major player in the world of financial software. He supplied the software for all the major stock exchanges around the world, and had built the most commonly used trading platform for hedge funds and stockbrokers. I asked Steve what he hoped to gain by floating, and he blushed slightly as he told me he had met his future wife, and wanted to be able to devote time, and money, to his new life as a husband, rather than all his money being tied up in his company, and his time devoted to micro-managing every aspect of it. He wanted some spare cash, and to take a director's role, rather than be an owner.

Lunch flew by as I outlined how a flotation worked, what he could expect in terms of the process, and how we would partner with our preferred accountants, and an investment bank, to oversee the process. I explained how we would set up a new board of directors and arrange the legal side of the new PLC. Before our meeting ended, I promised to type up some bullet points, and email him all the information. I also arranged to email some projections based on his last three years accounts, so he could decide whether a flotation would generate the cash he wanted.

"I can see why Ivan rates you so much," he said, surprising me, "I can tell you know your stuff. I'll wait for your email, and once I know where we are money wise, I'll be instructing. I won't bother speaking to any other law firms now."

I smiled widely."Good, I look forward to hearing from you," and paid the bill before heading back to my office. As soon as I got back, I called our contact at Deloitte, and asked for the projections. I found information about the pros and cons of floating a company, and saved them, ready to add to the projections when they came in. I had worked on a flotation during my traineeship, so was pretty familiar with the processes. Just to be sure, I nipped along to my old office to speak to Matt, who was quite the expert, and who had handled a lot of flotations for the firm. He checked over the info I was planning to send to Steve, and added a few notes of his own, so a complete package would go over.

Back in my office, my phone rang. "Good afternoon Elle, did you have a good weekend?" Ivan's sultry voice purred at me. "The girls missed you yesterday, almost sulked when they realised they had to put up with just me for the day."

"I doubt that very much Ivan, can't see those little girls sulking over anything, especially given the way you dispense sausages."

"Have you never seen a spaniel sulk? I can assure you that they do."

I laughed, "I hope you gave them a cuddle from me. Anyway, what can I do for you today?"

"I'm negotiating a deal for a controlling interest in a telecoms company. I may need heads of agreement drawn up fast. Are you free today at all? I can run through the points I'm negotiating to give you a head start on the contract."

I checked my schedule. "Can do six onwards today."

"Ok. I'll pick you up at six from your office. We'll go eat."

"Great, see you then." *Bugger, there goes my manicure and waxing appointment.* I went out to Laura's office and asked her to cancel my beauty appointments, and put Ivan in my diary at six. I spent the rest of the afternoon with another new client who wanted some corporate structure work done. I just about had time to email Steve Robbins the projections from Deloitte and explanations I'd promised him, before Ivan arrived.

As usual, my brain fried slightly at the sight of him. He'd had his hair trimmed at the weekend, but it was still floppy, and slightly messy. He was wearing a dark grey suit, with a white shirt, and a deep charcoal tie. Knowing how muscular he was underneath the urbane exterior made me shiver slightly.

"Are you cold?" He asked, "the air con is up quite high in here." *Damn, he noticed.*

"No, I'm fine thanks. Where would you like to go eat?"

"I'll surprise you."

His hand rested in the small of my back as we walked through reception to the lifts. Priti raised an eyebrow and gave me a wide smile as I bid her goodnight. Outside, the Bentley was waiting, and I slid onto the buttery soft leather seat, before fishing around in my bag for my notebook and pen.

"Shall we do the notes for the contract now and get it out of the way?" I asked Ivan.

He proceeded to list out the points of negotiation, the figures he was aiming for, and the terms he was demanding. I could effectively write a head of agreement with that information, and simply amend any changes on the fly if needed. By the time we finished, the car pulled up. I peered out of the window to see where we were, and discovered we were outside Claridges. The doorman opened my door, while Ivan's bodyguard opened his, and we made our way inside.

We sat in the bar and had a gin and tonic before being shown to our table. Ivan seemed a little edgy, his eyes sweeping the room before we sat at the table. His security were stationed just outside the restaurant, which seemed to make him nervous.

"We don't have to eat here if it's making you edgy," I said, frowning.

"It's fine, I'm just not used to them being out of the room," he admitted, "I'm just being a girl."

I told him I'd had a pay rise, and a load of new clients thanks to him, and he seemed pleased, until I mentioned that Oscar had instructed us too.

"I thought you told him to leave you alone?" He looked cross.

"I did, but I also said that if we are in a professional setting, then he was to be polite. He's going to be a client, I can't tell him to piss off. I'll make sure he keeps his hands to himself."

"Hmm, sneaky. Take Roger tomorrow night, so at least you have someone with you."

"Is that alright? I don't want to keep nicking your driver."

"It's no trouble at all. I have several drivers and security people, sparing one to ensure your safety is no issue. I'd have one with you 24/7 if you'd let me." I pulled a face.

"No thanks. I doubt very much that anyone's bothered about assassinating little old me, apart from Marion Smith."
Ivan laughed. "She is out on bail, probably wants to poke you in the eye with her knitting needle."

I laughed, "So why did you buy that company? I thought you were mainly into corporate finance?"

He looked quizzical, "No, telecoms primarily, I own mainly communications companies, although I do quite a lot of venture capital these days too. I bought the engineering firm because they manufacture the cables I use. I get a hell of a cost saving through owning it. I own the 'Talk 'n' Walk' network."

"Priti thought you were only into venture capital and corporate finance. Shows what she knows. I had no idea. Are all the T&W shops yours too?" He nodded.

"My biggest company is the Russian one. We're the biggest comms company in Russia and the old Soviet Union countries. Fair sized on the African continent too. You need to start googling people Elle, you should know all this," he chided.

"I thought Priti was the human equivalent of google. I'll stop listening to her in future," I said, embarrassed. He smiled, and leaned over to squeeze my hand.

"So do you have any free time this week?"

"So far, just after lunch on Wednesday. Mind you, I need to try and schedule some beauty appointments. Nobody wants a yeti as their lawyer."

"Are you free Saturday night?"

"Yes, why?"

"I have a function I need to attend, and I'd like you to join me. There will be several CEOs attending, so it would be a good networking opportunity for you. It's a fundraiser at the Grosvenor, you'll enjoy it."

"I see. I'm going to struggle to shop for a dress. It's rather short notice." I didn't say no, but was panicking inside about affording a dress, given that my pay rise didn't kick in until the following month. *Steel yourself to say thank you if he offers to buy you a dress. Swallow your pride girl.*

"I'm booking you on Wednesday. We will do the negotiation, then go shopping. If I can persuade a salon to open late, we can get your treatments done. How does that sound?" I smiled.

"Sounds good. I'll have your contract ready by Wednesday morning at the latest, so we should be good to go directly after lunch."

"Does that mean you'll accompany me on Saturday night?"

"Yes, I'd be delighted to."

Ivan looked really pleased, and seemed to relax in front of me. Our first course arrived, and we began to eat. I contemplated seeing him in black tie for the first time. I'd probably combust on the spot.

"You have a strange look on your face, Elle. Is everything all right?" Ivan asked, frowning slightly.

"Yeah, I'm good thanks. Food's delicious." *Oh god, does this man not miss a thing? Cool down girl.* He stared at me as if he was trying to read my mind. "Do you have a girlfriend Ivan?" I asked. If we were going to be spending time together, even as friends or colleagues, I needed to know.

"Not really. I date occasionally, but nobody special. Nobody I'd care to spend a Sunday with, put it that way."

"I see, so I was honoured?"

"You were indeed. I enjoyed our day together. Did you?"

I paused, "yes, I did. It was fun." It had also made me forget my humiliation at Oscar's hands, but I didn't say that.

"I feel relaxed with you. There's not many women I can say that about," he said, surprising me.

"Why aren't you usually relaxed with women?" I asked, frowning.

"Most of the time they're with me purely for what they can get, either that, or it's because of what I stand for, money and power. It makes me suspicious of people."

"You don't say," I teased, "says Mr I'll-buy-you-a-dress-and-get-your-legs-waxed. Have you ever considered that women fall at your feet because of your pretty face?"

He roared with laughter, "you're priceless sometimes. I know full well that if you already had a suitable dress, you wouldn't even allow me to shop with you. As it is, I know the prices will have to be hidden from you, or you'll be offering to pay me back. I'm glad you think I'm pretty though. It's high praise coming from you." I looked at him quizzically. "Elle, has it not occurred to you that you have the two wealthiest men in the Canary Wharf tower following you around like puppy dogs? There's only one more billionaire in that tower, and I don't think you've met him yet, which is a good thing. Three ensnared hearts is too much for any girl." *Ensnared hearts? Quite an admission Ivan.*

"I shall have to engineer a meeting. I always was a greedy girl," I quipped, Ivan just looked amused.

"Now THAT statement surprises me. You come across as very self contained. I can't imagine you being needy or clingy."

"No, you're right, I'm not. I'm very ordinary though, and I can't see what you and Oscar find so fascinating." Ivan just shook his head, looking amused. Our next course arrived, and we chatted about the food, which was exceptional, and the company Ivan was looking to take over. Dinner seemed to pass in a flash, and all too soon we were back in the car heading back to Canada Square.

Chapter 2

We pulled up outside my flat, and I invited Ivan in for coffee. Thankfully, his security detail stayed outside in the car, and we made our way up. Ivan sat at the kitchen island as I made our drinks, looking around the apartment. "This is a lovely flat Elle. Very secure too. You have a flatmate, is that right?"

"Yes. It belongs to James. He's away working in the States at the moment. I just rent a room from him. I love it here, it's very peaceful."

"This James, what's he like?"

"Oh, he's lovely. Looks like a bear, all hairy and scruffy, but he's very intelligent and sweet. He's a great cook too, keeps me well fed when I'm working. We're great friends."

"You're not involved with him?" I shot Ivan a 'don't be daft look', before placing his latte in front of him.

"Surely your background check told you that the only man I've been involved with recently was Oscar, and you know what happened there. I can't possibly manage more than one man at a time, given that I work stupid hours."

"We only found three men, including Oscar. I'm assuming there are gaps in your relationship history on the check we did," Ivan said.

"No, there's no gaps," I replied, blushing slightly. *Yeah ok, just three men, not exactly experienced.* Ivan looked shocked, but didn't say anything. I decided to change the subject. "Where do you live when you're in London?"

"Not far, I have an apartment in Saffron wharf. There's a garden square nearby for the girls. They prefer the woods, but it would have meant a long commute each day." He paused, as if trying to find the right words to say something. "Elle, can I ask you something?"

"Sure, fire away."

He looked a bit pained, "when I said we would have raw, wild sex, did that scare you off?" His eyes bored into me, and I knew I'd have to tell the truth.

"Yes, it did. It made me feel like a sex object, or a plaything. I'm not experienced enough yet to take on a sex god, and I don't want to sleep my way up the career ladder, I'm sorry." I stared into my coffee, feeling a bit stupid.

"No, Elle, I'm sorry if I made you feel that way. Very Russian of me, sometimes I forget..." He trailed off.

"Forget what?"

"That you're not the sharp, assertive lawyer when you're off the clock," he said, "and that you are a lady. I bet I scared the life out of you."

"It sounded...rough. That's what turned me off. I'm really not into the whole 'pain is sexy' thing."

"I see." *Did I detect disappointment in his eyes?* I cleared away our cups, making it clear that coffee was over. Ivan didn't seem to take the hint.

"I'm gonna send you home now. I need my sleep." I said, thinking that possibly, direct was better. Ivan stood and smiled warmly.

"Sleep well. I'll see you Wednesday afternoon. I'll make all the arrangements." He gently kissed my cheek, sending hormones flying around my body, and left.

I lay in bed that night replaying our evening. I tried to analyse what was holding me back with Ivan. We got along well, I fancied the pants off of him, but the idea of actually having sex with him terrified me. I felt overwhelmed by him, both physically and mentally, as if there would be no way back once I experienced making love with him, and I would measure all men by him for evermore. In addition, he was a client, and the last thing I wanted was a reputation at work.

I woke up at my usual time, and left for the gym at six sharp. I needed to get in early and make a start on the contract for Ivan, before my first meeting at nine thirty. I noticed I needed more tights, and decided I would have to get over my squeamishness and ask Laura to pick some up for me. I had always regarded women who claimed to be too busy to do the normal stuff in life to simply be disorganised. There was no way I'd get the chance to go anywhere near a shop today, my schedule was packed, and as it was, I'd be doing my laundry at eleven that night so that I didn't run out of clean knickers that week.

I was at my desk by seven fifteen, and began the contract, working through my notes carefully and methodically. In the end, I finished it by quarter past nine, and emailed it over to Ivan. Approximately two minutes later my phone rang.

"How have you done this by quarter past nine?" Ivan asked.

"Good morning Ivan, hope you're well. I got up early," I replied, "besides, I have a busy day ahead, so I thought I'd get it done and out of the way. Let me know what amendments I need to make. By the way, I'm going to need Roger at half seven, is that ok?"

"Yes fine, I'll tell him. I'll let you know about the contract." He cut the call. *So rude.* I was interrupted by the arrival of Laura with a cup of tea, and a sheaf of faxes that had come through for me to look through. I skimmed through quickly before my nine thirty turned up.

Paul Lassiter was the owner/CEO of a recruitment company. He was tall, blonde and boyish looking. While not quite in Ivan's league, he had a warm smile, and was extremely charming. He explained that he wanted to separate his temp, permanent and training divisions, and needed an umbrella company set up, preferably in a low tax territory, and the three new companies set up to funnel their revenue through the parent firm. I made copious notes, and promised to do some research and email him with some proposals. I explained that I would need to speak to our partner accountants to make sure that nothing would fall apart under the scrutiny of HMRC, should they decide to look.

As soon as he left, I called Lewis to pick his brain. He explained the best way to set it all up, and promised to email all the paperwork over. With that issue dealt with, I grabbed my bag, and zipped down to Smollenskis for lunch with another prospective client. The afternoon saw yet another meeting, this time with Steve Robbins, who, on seeing the projections from Deloitte, had decided to go ahead with the flotation. Matt joined us, and set everything in motion, with the date set for early July, to give everyone time to complete the necessary steps. Steve left happy, the prospect of several million quid, and a change of pace, in time for his wedding in August, was enough to put a huge smile on his face. Matt was to actually handle most of the work for the float, with me sitting in to learn how he managed it. He promised to update me daily on his progress.

I gulped down another cup of tea, while I checked, and replied to the day's emails. The next time I looked up, it was half six. I switched off my screen, and pulled my bags onto my shoulder. I was overjoyed to see Roger waiting outside. It was only five minutes' walk to the flat, but I was late, and my bags were heavy.

Back home, I had a super quick shower, applied fresh makeup, and dressed in five minutes. I hopped in the lift, and knocked on Oscar's door at precisely half seven.

I felt a momentary pang of regret on seeing him again. He still looked like my Oscar, as he smiled, rather nervously, at me. He was wearing a dark navy suit, with a dark blue shirt, and matching tie. He looked great. I mentally slapped myself to remind me that he was no longer my boyfriend, and was a secret homosexual, who felt that women were either brood mares or playthings.

"Hi Elle, you look lovely. I booked us into Nobu. Hope that's ok," he said.

"Super, thank you. Shall we set off? Our car is waiting downstairs," I replied.

In the lift, I tried not to breathe in his cologne, knowing the effect it used to have on me. I could feel the tension radiating off of Oscar in waves, as if he was nervous of our meeting.

Roger hopped out of the Mercedes, and opened the door for me. Once we had settled into our seats, and set off, I pulled out my notebook. "Shall we make a start on the governance issues you want us to take over?"

Oscar seemed to relax a little, as he outlined the work that the bank would require. As it was a privately owned bank, it wasn't as heavily regulated as a PLC, but still had to comply with banking codes, and general company law.

"Are you contributing to the LIBOR figures?" I asked.

"Yes we do. Each day a team member sends the calculation. We are the banks bankers, so we also calculate the overnight rates." I gaped at him.

"I thought the Bank of England did that?"

"No, they are the lender of last resort, we are the day to day bankers for NatWest, Barclays etc. The only other comparable banks are Rothschilds, and Goldman Sachs."

"I see. Are your reporting procedures transparent on that? What I mean is, could there ever be an accusation of price fixing?"

Oscar frowned, "well, yes, I suppose we could be accused of it, but they'd have to prove it went on. If that happened, we'd just deny it."

We arrived at Nobu, and were shown to our table. Looking at the menu, I had no idea what to choose, so I asked Oscar to order for me. He picked a starter I couldn't even pronounce, and black cod for my main, with a bottle of white wine that I'd never heard of. We carried on with our discussion, me making copious notes, and Oscar listing out the points confidently and knowledgeably. We finished just before our main courses arrived.

My cod was gorgeous, I groaned slightly as the flavours hit my taste buds. "Nice?" Oscar asked, smiling at me, "it's their signature dish."

"Fabulous," I replied, pleased that he'd ordered it for me. He put down his knife and fork for a moment, and looked at me.

"Mother came to see you."

"She did. Why did you tell her what happened? You should have kept it quiet. She didn't need to know the nasty details."

He sighed. "She was so sure that you were at fault, that maybe you were just a gold digging little social climber after all, and a few other nasty comments. I flipped out and told her exactly what had happened. Ruined her illusion that I could never do any wrong. Also changed her perception of you somewhat. She thinks you walk on water now."

"It doesn't matter what she thinks anymore. Anyway, if she hears what happened to Marion Smith, she may well just start hating me again." Oscar looked quizzical. "I uncovered a huge fraud at Ivan's firm when I was doing some work there. Hauled her in front of Ivan who frightened her so much, she wet herself. It wasn't good." To my surprise, Oscar started laughing.

"Ivan didn't tell me about that. Mother did mention that Mrs Smith had been asked to leave the women's institute committee, but she didn't say why. I bet Ivan freaked, given how squeamish he is." *What?*

"So has your mum forgiven you now?" I asked.

"I think so. When she came back from seeing you, she cried. Asked if she'd made me unhappy, and asked if I wanted to 'come out' as gay." I looked at him expectantly. "I'm not gay, Elle, it was a bad habit Darius and I got into, but being caught shook us both up. He is terrified Arabella will find out, and I was terrified that it would ruin my life. So I reassured her that I'm hetero, and it was just an aberration. I think she's ok now."

"She was worried about you. Not because she thought you were gay, but because she thought you were hurting. You look fine now though," I said.

"I'm anything but fine Elle, I miss you more than you would ever believe. I need to ask you something, and I don't want you to get angry."

"Go on."

"Are you with Ivan now?"

I shook my head. "No I'm not. We really are just friends and colleagues at the moment. I think he wants more, but I'm not ready. Both of you seem to forget that I'm not experienced with men, and I'm not terribly adept at coping with alpha males." Oscar looked like he let out a huge breath. "I don't know why it matters to you though, I can't be with you."

"I just want you to be happy Elle, and if helping you be successful at work does that for you, then I'm glad to be of service. It also means I still get to see you, even if it is only business." He looked so sad that my heart broke a little bit for him.

"I meant what I said Oscar, only business. I don't think you realise how much you hurt me. It's better I still have my head held high, and my integrity intact. I can't be with you knowing what I saw, and after hearing you trying to buy my silence. I'll always care about you, but I'm too ordinary to be with someone like you. I live in a different world, with different rules. I hope you understand that."

"Yes I do understand, my only hope is that you change your mind, and come back to me." I didn't reply. I actually didn't want to rule anything out, although I also didn't want to rush back to him. It was far better to let time provide the answer.

By the time we left the restaurant, we were at least friends again. Roger drove us home, and Oscar exited the lift at his own floor. I didn't want to put temptation in my way by inviting him up for coffee, nor did I want to lead him on. I also had to do some laundry, and pack my gym bag for the next morning. I was practically asleep on my feet.

I had no sooner put a wash on when my phone rang "you alone?" Ivan barked.

"Yes, did you expect something else?" I asked, annoyed. "Was there something you needed?"

"No. Still ok for one tomorrow?"

"Yes of course," I replied, "why wouldn't I be?"

"See you then," said Ivan, before ringing off abruptly. I stood staring at the phone, marvelling at the rudeness of the man.

It was almost midnight by the time I fell into bed, physically and mentally exhausted from the demands of the day.

At half five, my alarm went off, rousing me from a deliciously deep sleep. I practically had to drag myself out of bed, and neck two cups of tea to get me moving. By the time I'd finished my workout, I was feeling better, and I made my way to the nineteenth floor for my breakfast meeting with Paul Lassiter.

His office was smaller than either Ivan's or Oscar's, and fairly ordinary. His assistant had provided us with croissants and coffee while we ran through Lewis' proposals and costings. I noted down the points he wanted clarified, and he decided that as soon as he was happy with those, he would give us the go-ahead.

"So are you seeing Ivan Porenski then?" Paul asked.

"No, I'm his lawyer, well one of them."

"I was under the impression that you were his girlfriend, he warned me not to ask you out," he said, giving me his boyish smile.

"Did he now? Maybe it was his very Russian way of keeping me safe from a charmer," I grinned to let him know I was teasing.

"He uses that 'I'm a Russian' thing way too much to get away with it with me. So tell me Elle, do I have to compete with him for your attention?"

I laughed, "I'm so busy right now that I'm struggling to give anything or anyone other than work my attention."

"I'll be waiting in the wings if you get a spare evening, and require some entertaining company," he said, smiling warmly. I stood to leave, and shook his hand, feeling a tingle shoot right up my arm. *Static?*

As I made my way back to my office, I thought about Paul. I liked him, and found him charming and nice. He didn't have the extraordinary charisma of Ivan, or the urbane sophistication of Oscar, but he seemed friendly and warm. I made a mental note to google him, having made the mistake of not doing my research before.

The rest of the morning zipped past in a blur of meetings, papers, and phone calls. Laura came in to let me know it was time to leave for my lunch meeting with yet another client. I checked my makeup before trotting down to the Italian bistro on the ground floor to schmooze a rather rotund CEO, who made full use of my expense account before instructing me for a real estate purchase.

At five to one, I raced up to Ivan's office, and arrived just before the other party. As usual, I sat quietly and made notes, as Ivan negotiated for their company. One of the figures quoted by the other party sounded wrong, I glanced up at Ivan to see if he'd picked it up, but it appeared that he'd missed it. Lifting my pad slightly so the other party couldn't see, I wrote a note, and the equation he'd missed, then I nudged his foot. He glanced over at the pad I was holding, and carried on, not missing a beat.

When he corrected the figure the other party had quoted, there was a murmur around the room. "I know you were under the impression that 120 million represented 60% of your company, but I can assure you that from your share price, it computes to 67%. Would you like time to check the figures?"

They all shook their heads, resigned to the fact that the amended figures were correct. As soon as Ivan finished the negotiation, we went straight to his office to update the contract I'd written. "I have never, ever met anyone quicker at maths than me. I can't believe I missed that. A stupid mistake that could have cost me millions. Fuck." He paced around the office angrily as I typed quickly to amend the parts that needed changes. Even though he wasn't angry with me, it still felt like I was locked in a room with a rather cross and growling lion. He even lapsed into Russian at one point, banging his fist on the desk, and I presume, letting out a string of foreign swear words.

"Would you mind allowing me to concentrate please?" I asked sweetly. He stared at me for a moment before sitting down opposite and staring sulkily out of the window. Thankfully, I finished fairly quickly, and I pressed 'print' with a sigh of relief. Ten minutes later, the agreements were all signed, and the meeting ended. As Ivan appeared to be in a foul mood, I decided to abort the shopping trip. I didn't fancy an afternoon walking on eggshells, and thought it would be better if I disappeared and looked for a dress after work.

Maybe we'll go shopping another time, I can see you're angry," I said, grabbing my handbag, and standing up to leave.

"Don't leave, I'm not angry with you"

"You just spent the last half hour sulking and swearing. It won't be a fun afternoon if you sit there with a face on you."

"A face on you? What does that mean?" The corners of his mouth twitched.

"It's a south London phrase for looking pissed off," I clarified.

"I think that seeing you dressed in couture will cheer me up. Come, let's go spend some money. You just saved me around 20 million quid, you deserve a treat."

The personal shopper at Harrods was a delightful middle aged lady, with an eye for detail and a superb changing room manner. We were installed in a suite, a comfy sofa for Ivan, and a roomy changing area for me. Ivan described the event we were attending, and after sweeping her eyes over my figure, she left to fetch a selection of dresses. The first couple I tried on were lovely, but when I stepped out to show Ivan, he pulled a face. "She needs something extraordinary, something that shows off her beautiful figure," said Ivan. She brought out another two dresses, one a deep red, fitted, and with origami style ruching down the bodice. It was impossibly glamorous, and looked extremely expensive. The other dress was champagne coloured, with hand sewn crystals embedded all over it. I loved the strapless design, with it's built in corset to pull my waist tight, and prevent the dress from slipping down. Ivan also liked both dresses.

"Let me try the red one again, and I'll make a choice," I said.

"No need, have both. Now, she needs shoes and bags to match them." The shopper scurried off.

"I don't need both," I protested.

"You look lovely in them, like a work of art. I want you to have them."

"Thank you."

Matching high heels were brought for me to try, and a selection of clutch bags. I made my choices, and they were taken to be wrapped. I made the assumption that we were all done.

"We still have an hour and a half till your appointment in the spa," said Ivan, "new lingerie? Work outfits? What would you like?"

"I couldn't possibly allow you to buy me lingerie," I flirted.

"In case I demanded to see you wearing it?" He looked lecherous.

"Er, yes."

"Work outfits it is then." We walked through to desk to pay for our purchases. Ivan made me stand away so I didn't find out the prices. I heard him asking the sales lady for directions to the department for women's day wear. We were quickly whisked into another suite, and racks of suits, blouses and day dresses were brought in. I tried each outfit on, with Ivan giving a yes or no. By the time we were done I had five new suits, three dress/jacket combos, seven tops, five pairs of shoes, and a new Prada handbag.

"I feel thoroughly spoilt," I said, smiling at Ivan on our way up to the urban retreat.

"You deserve it. I like buying you things. You look cute in those suits."

"I'm supposed to look businesslike, not cute."

"Alright, you look business like and sophisticated in those cute little suits. Better?"

I giggled. "Yes, I suppose. What have you booked me into the spa for?"

"Nails, feet and waxing. I didn't know whether you wanted a Brazilian or a Hollywood though," said Ivan, looking sly, "so I said you'd choose when you got there. So for future reference, what should I have booked?" *Nosy bastard. Think I'm falling for that one?*

"Well I normally have a vajazzle, I'm sure they won't mind extending the appointment a little." His mouth dropped open in astonishment before he twigged that I was teasing.

"You're winding me up aren't you?"

"Yes I am, you nosy bugger."

"Touché Elle, touché"

The spa was an oasis of luxury at the top of Harrods. What made it even more luxurious was the 'express' service, that meant I had four therapists working on me at the same time, to give me the fastest, most perfect French mani/pedi I'd ever had. They even had four of those uv lamp thingies so there was no waiting time at all.

I was relieved to get my waxing done. Although I was fair, I hated hair on my legs, and had been sorely tempted to shave. My waxer was fast and skilled, barely hurting me at all, so after a relatively ok experience with my underarms, I went for a Brazilian. "Holy shit, that smarts," I yelped, as she ripped the wax off.

"We have to suffer to be beautiful for our men," she trilled cheerfully, "you can't stop now honey, you'd be lopsided." I looked down. One side was bald, the other, like an overgrown hedge.

"Go for it," I said, gritting my teeth. The next time I looked, she was trimming a little landing strip. It looked bizarre.

"No hot baths, swimming, tight clothes or sex for the next 24 hours please. You don't want infected follicles."

I dressed, and walked back to reception. Ivan had booked himself a massage while I was being tortured, and looked relaxed and happy. "My place or yours for dinner? We can take something in or get it delivered."

"I don't mind," I said, "wherever you like."

"Can we have dinner at mine tonight? I've not seen the girls all day."

"Sure." We went down to the food hall and Ivan picked out some Moroccan food, flatbreads, and some patisserie, and laden with goodies, we headed back to the docklands.

Ivan's apartment was enormous. It was the penthouse to a large block, slightly further down the river from mine, and had a large outside terrace, albeit one with very high, Perspex edging.

"Bulletproof, and dog proof," Ivan explained. Bella and Tania were overjoyed to see him, jumping all over him as soon as he sat down. He gave each of them a kiss, before switching the oven on to heat up our food, and pouring two glasses of wine.

"Where did your guards go?" I asked.

"Security room, and the floor below is where they live when they're off duty. It's still heavily protected here. Gotta keep my girls safe, eh girls?" They both wagged their tails, and gazed at him with devotion.

We ate outside on the terrace. It was a beautiful summer evening, one of those where the river shimmered, and the air hung heavy and still. After the madness of my week, it was like an oasis of calm. The dogs sat our feet, playing with rawhide bones, and Ivan put Adele on the music system.

He told me stories of growing up in Moscow, tales of such hardship and destitution that my heart clenched for him. He described the arduous journey to England, and the difficulties he had when he got here. It felt as though he was baring himself to me, showing me the man inside the pretty packaging, and asking me to understand him.

In turn, I told him about growing up on the estate, of not fitting in, and of my desperate desire to escape. I told him my fears of never being good enough, of being poor, and the lengths I went to, in order to cover up my lack of sophistication.

"Let me hold you, beautiful girl," he said, holding his arms out for me. I sank into his warm embrace, and breathed in his lovely scent. He felt solid and strong, as if he could keep me safe forever. He pulled me onto his lap, and just held me, one hand lightly caressing my spine, as we sat in a strange embrace.

"Please let me kiss you," he whispered, pulling back from me slightly so he could look at me. I gazed into his sapphire eyes for a moment, before closing mine, and leaning forward to gently graze his soft, full lips with mine.

Our kisses were light and soft at first, before growing firmer and deeper. His tongue pushed into my mouth to meet mine, shyly at first, growing bolder, until he was claiming full control of my mouth, kissing me hard, as his tongue stroked mine. His hands roamed over my shoulders, and down my spine, sending a delicious shiver right through my body which ended in my groin.

"Are you cold baby?" He asked. I shook my head, I was practically melted in a mush of hormones, and although making out felt rather adolescent, I was enjoying the slowness of it. I went back in for more kisses.

Eventually I pulled away, "I need to go home."

"Please stay, I really need to make love to you tonight."

"I can't, not tonight. Another night." I didn't want to spell out that it was time of the month.

"Why not?" He looked concerned. "Don't you want to?"

"Oh yes, I want to. By Saturday, all will be fine."

He twigged, " oh ok, I see. Saturday it is then. I'll pick you up at six, and I honestly can't wait." He kissed me again, a deep, needy kiss, before Roger took me, and all my bags home.

Chapter 3

I was in the office bright and early the following morning, due to having to forego my swim. I fired up my screen to check my emails, and make a start on my paperwork. An email from Ivan popped into my inbox. Smiling, I opened it.

From: Ivan Porenski
To: Elle Reynolds
2nd June 2013
Subject: Is it Saturday yet?

Elle,

I'm sure it's Saturday today. My secretary tells me it's only Thursday. Is she lying?

Am about to combust

Ivan xx

I replied quickly.

From: Elle Reynolds
To: Ivan Porenski
2nd June 2013

Subject: re Is it Saturday yet?

Ivan

It's only 8 hours since I last saw you. Premature anticipation a problem for you? ;)

Elle x

I pressed send, and carried on replying to Paul Lassiter about his umbrella company. My inbox pinged again.

From: Ivan Porenski
To: Elle Reynolds
2nd June 2013
Subject: re re Is it Saturday yet?

Elle

Anticipation, premature or otherwise, is always the best bit. ;)

Ivan xx

I replied quickly.

From: Elle Reynolds
To: Ivan Porenski
2nd June 2013
Subject: re re re Is it Saturday yet?

Ivan

I'm sincerely hoping the eventual conclusion will be far better than the anticipation. ;) now, I need to get on with my work. I have some extremely demanding clients to keep happy.

Elle xx

Twenty seconds later, my inbox pinged again

From: Ivan Porenski
To: Elle Reynolds
2nd June 2013
Subject: re re re re Is it Saturday yet?

Elle

Nobody demanding as much as me I hope?

Ivan xx

I was too wrapped up in getting the information Paul required, sent to him, to reply to Ivan straightaway. I had quite literally just pressed 'send' when my phone rang. It was Ivan. "Hello beautiful, you didn't reply to my last email?"

"I was just about to. I was just doing a work one, I can truthfully say that you are definitely my most demanding client."

"But am I your favourite client?"

"You most certainly are."

"I don't want to wait till Saturday to see you."

"I have a full schedule till then. Plus, you know, it's not a good time."

"I know. Well have a good day, and call me if you have some spare time."

"Will do. Speak to you later."

I hugged myself with glee. Only two days to go. Kissing last night seemed to have broken my apprehension about getting physical with him. I'd even had a spin with my trusty B.O.B to ease some of the sexual tension last night so I'd been able get off to sleep. I was wearing one of my new outfits, and carrying my new Prada bag. Life really did feel pretty good.

I spent most of the morning with Mr Carey, going through the governance issues we were tackling for Oscar. I expressed my concerns about the LIBOR reporting, and he suggested daily website posting of the rate they calculated, so that the process was seen to be transparent. I called Oscar, and suggested it.

"Easy enough to do. I do wonder why you're worrying about it though. It's never even been mentioned in the press. I doubt anyone even knows what it is. If it makes you happier though, we'll start it today."

"There's a lot of anti-bank sentiment around, so I wouldn't be surprised if it came under scrutiny at some point. As long as you're seen to be transparent, it should head off problems further down the line." We went on to discuss the auditors, and the banking code changes that were coming into force. Oscar was impressed with Mr Carey's knowledge of audit protocols, and was happy to meet with him the following week to finalise the changeover to our company.

The day flew by in a flurry of meetings, culminating in taking a client out for dinner. She was the owner of a publishing company, and was negotiating the purchase of a rival. It was a different experience dealing with a woman, and I liked her enormously. She was meeting the other party the following Tuesday, and we agreed that I would attend with her. Thankfully, it wasn't a late finish, and I was able to get home by 9.30.

The flat felt empty without James, and the only item in the fridge was milk that I'd picked up on my way home from work. I sat in bed, with my laptop open, and googled Ivan. I read his Wikipedia page, and marvelled at the number of companies he controlled. Before I logged off, I clicked on images, to see page upon page of his beautiful face. I also saw the same woman in a lot of the pictures. She was tall, dark haired, and looked Slavic. Clicking on the links, I found out her name was Dascha Meranov, and was the daughter of another Oligarch. There were pictures of the two of them together from 2009 right through to the end of 2012. I studied her face before switching off the laptop, and dozing off.

I was grateful that Friday passed in a blur of busyness, and before I knew it, I was ensconced in Lauren's bar with my workmates, sipping a large glass of cold white wine. "It's been a hell of a week for you, Elle," said Peter, "you must be exhausted. Any plans for the weekend?"

"Out Saturday night to a ball, so tomorrow afternoon I have a hair appointment. That's about it. Nothing planned for Sunday, although I have a bit of paperwork to catch up on. What about you?"

"My girlfriends parents are coming to stay," he said, pulling a face, "is Golding taking you?"

"No, I'm accompanying Ivan. He said it would be good for networking. I'm not seeing Oscar anymore."

"But he instructed us?"

"Yes. That was after I stopped seeing him though."

"Did he instruct us so that he could hang around you?" *God you're sharp Peter.*

"There's always that possibility."

"So even when you dump them, they still hang around like devoted puppies?" I just smiled. "Jesus Elle, you're like Pearson Hardwick's secret weapon. What with Paul Lassiter making moon eyes too, we'll be roping off an area so they can form a queue soon."

"What's Paul Lassiter got to do with anything?" I frowned.

"There are three billionaires in the tower, Golding, Ivan, and Paul Lassiter, and all three of them are going stupid over you. Plus of course, all three are now Pearson Hardwick clients. Carey has been trying for years to get them signed up, and yet, even when you spit them out, they sign on the dotted line just to get to sniff your skirt. It's impressive."

"Has it occurred to you that they might actually think I'm good at my job? I saved Ivan a shitload of money on two occasions, and I wasn't even aware who Paul was. I don't think it's all about my sex appeal, it could well be my little brain too." I was getting annoyed. Peter was insinuating that I was getting new clients by being female and pretty. "The proof will be whether I can keep these clients happy. If it was just my pretty face, they'll move on to a better lawyer pretty sharpish. None of these people are fools Peter, and you're doing them a disservice assuming that they are."

"Oh, don't get me wrong, I don't think they're fools, not for one moment, I'm just saying that you managed to do what eluded Carey for years, and you made it look effortless. Whatever it is you've got, we need to clone it."

"Maybe the firm should recruit more female lawyers?"

Peter pulled a face, "they're normally more hassle than they're worth. I think we had a couple over the years, but they don't like the workload, or the long hours. They were never at their desks by 7.30 like you, nor did they land any clients. I don't think it's a female thing, although it doesn't hurt to have good looking people. Maybe it's a charisma thing." With that, he went off to get another drink.

I left the bar at ten, and was surprised to see Roger waiting patiently outside. "Mr Porenski asked that I see you home safely," he said, holding open the car door. *How did he know I was here?*

"Thanks Roger. Did you track my phone to find me?" Roger didn't answer, just pinked up slightly. I decided I needed to have words with Ivan about privacy, before sliding gratefully into the soft seat. My feet were aching from my new shoes, and I was shattered.

Back at the flat, I microwaved my meal for one, and switched on the telly. I flicked mindlessly through the channels, wondering what James was up to. I decided to give him a call.

"Elle! It's great to hear from you. How's everything?"

"Boring without you. How are they treating you out there?"

"Pretty good really. I have a nice apartment, and the team are ok. We're making good progress, although I can't wait to get home and work by myself again. I'd forgotten how much I hate office politics."

I laughed, "you wanna get a taste of mine sometime. Even the men are little divas at my place at times. Did you look at holidays?"

"Yep, I've booked two weeks in Spain. Nice hotel, on the beach, quite a quiet place. I keep meaning to email you the link so you can have a look. We both need some downtime by the sounds of it."

"Great. I honestly can't wait. I've not felt sand between my toes for years. Oh, by the way, did you shave your beard off?" The line went quiet, "James, are you still there?"

"Yes, I'm still here.....yes, I got rid of it."

"Oh take a photo and send it to me."

"Not yet. I'm still getting used to it. Soon."

"Okay. I promise I won't laugh or anything."

"I have no doubt you won't. I need to get on now, someone's waiting for me outside. Great to speak to you. See you soon yeah?"

"Yeah, you too. Bye." I cut the call, and switched the TV off, before flopping into bed. Tomorrow was the big day.

I did my usual workout on Saturday morning, before catching the eight o'clock yoga class. I was showered, dressed and done by half ten. I had an eleven o'clock doctor's appointment to get to, as I had decided to get a contraceptive shot. The last thing I wanted was a pregnancy to deal with, so it seemed like the best option. On my way back from the doctors, I even managed to stop off at the supermarket and stock up on food. I unpacked the shopping, and fixed a sandwich for lunch. My hair appointment was booked for three, so I had plenty of time to exfoliate, and apply a light tan first, as I wouldn't be able to shower again once my hair was done. Ivan had already text me to say he'd be picking me up at six thirty, as the event started at seven, and we had to get over to the West End.

I sat at the island, and flicked through a hair magazine as I ate my lunch. I had decided on the red dress, and as it wasn't strapless, was trying to decide whether to wear my hair up or down. I took a quick photo of the dress on its hanger to show the stylist, and get his advice. Idly, I wondered if the salon did makeup as well. My musings were interrupted by my phone chirping as a text arrived. It was Ivan enquiring whether I had decided which dress I was wearing. I quickly replied that I'd be wearing the red one. He didn't respond, which puzzled me slightly.

After lunch, I took a long bath, and spent a pleasant hour exfoliating and buffing, applying a hint of golden tan, and carefully applying primer to my face, so my makeup would look good later. I threw on a track suit, and walked over to the salon, which was on the ground floor of the arcade.

My stylist was a delightful little Italian man called Giuseppe, who, on seeing the photo of my dress, declared my hair should be put up in a soft, elegant chignon. As it had been washed that morning, he proceed to roll it up in heated curlers to set it in curls first. I asked about makeup, and another, very gay, Frenchman called Andre was brought over to be introduced. He made a start while my rollers were cooling down, and between the two of them, they worked some powerful magic.

The woman staring back at me in the mirror an hour later would rival any model who had previously graced Ivan's arm. Even in the scruffy track suit, I looked flawless, and sophisticated. I paid my bill, buying the lipstick Andre had used, and tipped them both generously. "Youra man won't know whatsa hit 'im," said Giuseppe, giving me a little hug.

I even stopped off at La Senza on my way home to pick up a red lace lingerie set. Tonight was very definitely the night. A shiver of excitement ran through me as I headed back to the flat.

I decided not to wear any jewellery other than a pair of small, gold earrings, mainly because I didn't own anything that would do the dress justice. With my hair and face done, all I had to do was put on my dress, underwear and shoes. It would only take five minutes, so I sat and had a coffee, and relaxed with a magazine for half an hour.

Ivan was a little early, I had only just stepped into my shoes, after zipping up my dress. I opened the door, and smiled as he just stood and stared at me. He looked amazing in his tuxedo, although to be fair, so did almost every man on the planet. "You look stunning Elle, I knew you'd look lovely, but I wasn't prepared for this," he said as he stepped into the flat. He twirled his index finger to indicate that I should turn around. "Beautiful, beyond breathtaking," he said, unable to take his eyes off me. I glowed under his praise, wanting to look my best for him. "I bought you a little something for tonight," he said, handing me a box. I took it over to the island, and opened it. I gasped as a trio of rubies sparkled at me. "I thought something to match your dress would be nice," he said, watching my face.

"They're lovely," I said, taking the necklace out of the box. Ivan stood behind me and did up the clasp. I did notice that his hands were shaking ever so slightly. I quickly took my earrings out, and replaced them with the ruby drops. Checking myself in the hall mirror, I really did look like a billionaire's girlfriend. I grabbed my clutch bag, and keys, and we set off.

Ivan helped me into the Bentley, making sure my dress was tucked in properly before closing the door. He slid into the seat beside me, and grasped my hand, smiling at me. "I really wasn't prepared for how fabulous you look tonight. Every man there will be envious of me having such a beautiful woman on my arm."

"You look pretty damn hot too. There's going to be a lot of envious women too." He leaned over, and kissed my cheek, being careful not to smudge my makeup.

He told me all about the charity on the way over. Apparently they helped children from disadvantaged backgrounds access further education and apprenticeships. "Good cause," I said softly.

"I think so too," he replied, "so tonight we find some nice auction lots, and outbid everyone. Does that sound like fun?"

"Depends what they are. I doubt if a signed football will really go with the decor in your office."

Ivan laughed, "and I doubt if you'd thank me for a signed rugby ball for yours. I'm hopeful we'll find something nice, and I can donate some money to the charity." He grinned. "Now, Elle, we will probably be photographed as we get out of the car. Just smile, and stay next to me. My security will prevent anyone getting too close."

"I wasn't planning on running off. Will security be with us all evening?"

"Oh yes. I don't go anywhere without them."

"Why is that?"

"Business in Russia is done differently to how it's done here. Any wealthy man is in constant danger, more so for Russians. The English settle disputes through the courts, Russians settle disputes with guns, or worse. There's no specific threat against me, so nothing for you to worry about."

"Don't you get fed up with the bodyguards trailing everywhere with you?" I was curious.

"No, I've had them so long that it just feels normal. I get nervous when they're not there."

"They weren't in the woods in Sussex, did that make you edgy?"

"They were there," he said, frowning, "they patrol the perimeter of my land constantly. Unless someone parachutes in, they can't get into the estate."

Our conversation ended as we pulled up at the entrance to the Grosvener. The doors were opened by uniformed attendants, and as soon as I stepped out of the car, the flashbulbs started, blinding me slightly. Within a heartbeat, Ivan was by my side, his arm firmly round my waist, his hand squeezing my hip. I kept my professional smile firmly stuck to my face, as Ivan paused to allow the press to photograph us, voices shouting out for him to tell them who I was. Ivan simply smiled, and remained silent before we turned and walked along the red carpet, and into the venue.

I breathed a sigh of relief that the blinding flashes had stopped. "You ok?" Ivan asked.

"Fine thanks. Glad that's over though, I couldn't see a thing." I still had spots in front of my eyes, but they were clearing. We were shown through to a large reception room, which was already filled with people. Ivan took two glasses of champagne from a passing waiter, and handed one to me. I sipped it gratefully, and looked around the room. The women all looked incredibly glamorous, and I was grateful for the dress Ivan had bought for me. I felt comfortable knowing I looked the part. People stood around chatting in groups, seeming to know one another.

"Come, there are some people I'd like you to meet," said Ivan, as he took my arm. As soon as we walked further in, he was accosted by various people who seemed delighted to see him. I was introduced to several CEO's, a few politicians, and two fairly famous actors, all of whom seemed to want to be Ivan's best friend.

I watched carefully as Ivan slipped on a 'public' persona. He was friendly and personable, but seemed to place himself at arms length, projecting a cool detachment to the people around us. It was fascinating to observe.

I was chatting to one of the actors, asking him about his latest role, when I felt Ivan's grip around my waist tighten. I looked up to see Oscar walk in with an impossibly beautiful brunette on his arm. I glanced at Ivan to reassure him that I wasn't bothered, and saw that Ivan was grim faced, and shooting daggers at Oscar. It was at that moment the woman moved into view, and I realised it was Dascha, and Ivan didn't look at all happy about her being Oscar's date. My stomach sank.

Oscar caught sight of me, and stared blatantly for a moment, before bringing Dascha over to introduce us. I figured the whole thing was a ploy to make me jealous, so instead, I smiled sweetly, and complimented Dascha profusely on her dress.

"Thank you, yours is lovely too," she purred in a heavily accented voice, "Ivan chose it for you no doubt? I can spot his taste a mile away. He always did buy such beautiful gifts." *Bitch.* I smiled in reply, turning my attention back to the two men. I overheard Ivan growl at Oscar.

"What are you playing at?"

"The same as you. You have a problem?" Replied Oscar quietly, clearly hoping I wouldn't hear them.

"So how did you two meet?" I asked Dascha, keeping my smile going.

"Oh, we've been seeing each other a little while," she said, "did Oscar not mention me? Or do you only discuss business at your meetings? I understand that both Oscar and Ivan are *clients* of yours. Your company must be pleased you get to know your clients so well."

"We don't discuss personal things at our meetings, purely business. It's probably why Oscar never mentioned he had a beautiful girlfriend." Oscar looked horrified, his attempt to make me jealous was backfiring spectacularly. "By the way, Oscar, did you action the LIBOR reporting?" He looked relieved that I'd changed the subject, and began to tell me in detail the changes that had been made in line with my recommendations. I listened politely, with one ear trained on Ivan and Dascha's conversation. I noticed they had lapsed into Russian, I also caught the flirty tone to her voice, and coquettish body language. Ivan's grip on my waist loosened, and eventually fell away as he became engrossed in his conversation. I stood slightly awkwardly, wondering what to do. I was about to suggest I went home and left them to it, when we were called into the dining room.

Ivan actually walked into the room with Dascha, his hand resting on the small of her back as he guided her in. I followed behind feeling rather dejected, and wondered if I could slip away without anyone noticing. Spotting the ladies room, I ducked in, and locked myself in a stall while I figured out what to do. I felt totally out of my depth, and rather humiliated. I fingered the ruby necklace, and in a moment of clarity, realised I'd been bought and paid for, and as such, could be treated in any way that Ivan pleased. I made the decision to leave, and in the morning I would ask Roger to return all the items Ivan had bought for me. I just couldn't help feeling that I'd sold my soul to the devil in return for a ruby and a red dress.

After ten minutes, I came out of the stall, and looked at my reflection in the mirror. I looked like a lady. I lifted my chin defiantly, and walked out of the ladies and towards the exit.

Chapter 4

"Where do you think you're going?" Ivan called out, hurrying to catch up with me. "The dining room's the other way."

"I'm getting out of your way, and heading home," I said, "I'll speak to you in the morning." I tried to turn towards the exit, but Ivan grabbed my arm in a vice-like grip.

"Elle, what's got into you? I don't understand why you want to go."

"Ivan, you're not a stupid man. Did you really think you could ignore me to fawn all over your ex, and I wouldn't mind? I might not understand Russian, but I understand flirting. Now I suggest you let me go home, and you can go back in there and spend the rest of the evening with her."

"I don't want her, I want you."

"I'm sorry, I can't do this. Right now I feel bought and paid for, in a dress that you chose, in jewellery that is probably worth what I earn in a year, and that bitch rubbed my nose in it. I just want to go home and take it all off, and be myself again." I fought hard to control the tears that threatened to bubble up inside. I really didn't want to lose control.

"Elle, listen to me, I changed to Russian because I was telling her to behave, and to leave you alone. I told her that I was with you now, and I didn't appreciate her nasty remarks. As for my gifts, there are no strings attached, I bought them because I wanted to make you happy, not because I expected any payback. You are still you, despite how wonderful you look tonight. Please come back inside with me....please."

I thought about it, Ivan looked worried. "Promise me that we won't sit with her?"

He let out a breath, "I promise." He took my hand and led me into the vast dining room, and through to a round table. I was seated next to the actor I'd been speaking to earlier, and a pleasant looking, stylishly dressed, middle aged lady was seated next to Ivan. I noted wryly that she looked as if all her birthdays and Christmases had come at once.

Thankfully the starters hadn't arrived at that point, and we hadn't kept anyone waiting. Ivan picked up the card listing the auction lots, and leaned in so we could both read it.

Lot 1 A weekend in New York, courtesy of Hilton hotels

Lot 2 A one week stay in the Red Sea resort of Sharm El Sheik, courtesy of Four Seasons Hotel Group

Lot 3 A spa weekend for two, courtesy of Champneys.

Lot 4 A dinner party for six, catered in your home by chefs from Gordon Ramsey, Claridges.

Lot 5 Dinner with Stephen Fry

Lot 6 Lunch with Lord Sugar

Lot 7 A private tour, and lunch at the House of Lords, with Lord Golding.

Lot 8 A helicopter flight over London, courtesy of Battersea Helicopters ltd.

Lot 9 A weekend in Paris, courtesy of Eurostar.

Lot 10 A one year subscription to Quintessentially yours, courtesy of Quintessentially yours.

Ivan pulled a biro out of his inside pocket, and ticked the weekend in New York, the concierge subscription, the helicopter flight, and the spa weekend. "Anything you want?" He asked. I shook my head. He poured me a glass of wine, and tucked his pen back in his pocket. "Are you ok now?"

"Yeah, I'm ok," I said unconvincingly. I was starting to relax again, and the threatened tears had disappeared. Ivan patted my hand, and started speaking to the woman next to him, who looked delighted.

The actor next to me leaned in, "so do you work?"

"Yes, I'm a corporate lawyer."

"Oh wow, I'm playing a lawyer in a new series being filmed in the autumn. You can give me some pointers on how I should act." He droned on all through the starter, and into the main course. Thankfully he was interrupted by the lady seated next to Ivan, who leaned over to compliment my outfit, stating that she loved my dress.

"She looks beautiful doesn't she?" Ivan said to her. She nodded in agreement, and smiled warmly. "I must introduce the two of you, "Joan, this is my girlfriend Elle, a corporate lawyer at Pearson Hardwick. Elle, this is Joan Lester, managing director of Conde Nast." I leaned across Ivan and shook her hand.

As our main courses arrived, she said, "I'll talk to you later, I need an acquisitions expert, and Ivan has recommended you." She pulled a business card out of her clutch, and passed it to me. "If I don't get a chance, call me next week, and we'll have lunch."

The auction began after dinner. We turned around to face the stage, and I immediately spotted Oscar and Dascha sitting two tables in. Their body language indicated they'd had a row, both leaning away from each other. Oscar looked extremely pissed off.

Ivan didn't bid early on, in any of the lots, coming in at the end, and easily outbidding his competitors. The last lot on offer was the subscription to Quintessentially yours, an upmarket concierge service. Both Ivan and Oscar began to bid for it, the price edging higher and higher, with neither willing to give in. A bit horrified, I touched Ivan's arm, and getting his attention, shook my head. A public pissing contest between two billionaires was nothing more than a circus show for the room. Thankfully Ivan backed down, and Oscar won the lot. For the first time that evening, he looked mildly pleased.

"Why did you stop me?" Ivan asked.

"Because it was just a pissing contest, and it was giving everyone in the room a 'my dicks bigger than your dick' show." Ivan roared with laughter.

"You, my darling, are priceless, and so very clever." He kissed the tip of my nose.

The band started up, so we moved to the bar. Ivan had to get a member of his security team to fetch the drinks, as he seemed to be mobbed at every step. It seemed as though every man wanted to be his best friend, and every woman wanted to flirt. He kept his arm firmly clamped around my waist, and made a point of introducing me to everyone as his girlfriend. Oscar and Dascha kept their distance, although I did catch Oscar staring rather wistfully at me, his eyes travelling down to the red Jimmy Choos on my feet.

Paul Lassiter came over to say hello, and after kissing the back of my hand, prompting a scowl from Ivan, proceeded to chat to Ivan for ten minutes about executive search.

At eleven, Ivan leaned down and whispered in my ear, "ready to leave? I really want to get you alone." I nodded. We said our goodbyes, and flanked by security, swept out of the Grosvener and into the waiting car.

"Are we going back to my place?" I asked.

"No. Sussex. It won't take long at this time of night."

"Shouldn't you have asked me first, rather than assume?"

"Ok, will you come back to Sussex with me tonight?"

"Yeah ok," I replied, rather sulkily. The mood really didn't feel right for making love. I felt edgy and off centre. Ivan pressed a button to raise the privacy screen.

"Tell me honestly Elle, are you pissed off that Dascha flirted with me, or pissed off that Oscar was there with someone else?"

"I was pissed off because it looked like you and Dascha were flirting with each other. I didn't give a toss that Oscar brought her."

"That's alright then. I like you being jealous, I wouldn't like it if it was directed towards another man. Oscar in particular."

"What happened with you and Dascha?"

"Not much. Went out with her, let her spend my money, put up with her appalling manners, then finally dumped her when she kicked Bella."

I frowned, "why did she kick Bella?"

"She weed in Dascha's shoe. Bella's way of letting her know she didn't like her I think. Kicked her so hard I had to take her to the vet to make sure there was no damage. Would have killed poor little Bella if security hadn't dragged her off. I couldn't be with her after that."

"I'm not surprised. What kind of person hurts an animal like that?"

"A psychopath. I actually felt quite sorry for Oscar having to spend an evening with her, but she only likes rich men, so she was probably quite happy."

"He was leaning so far away from her, he was almost at the next table," I giggled, "Oscar has a lot of faults, but bad manners isn't one of them. He looked horrified when she insulted me."

"I saw. She was beside herself with jealousy over you, and because she doesn't really know who you are, she threw the only barbs she could find. She figured out that Oscar only invited her to rattle me, and try and make you jealous. She was livid about it, not being the centre of attention. Then when Paul slobbered over you, I thought she would actually turn green."

"Paul did not slobber over me. He kissed the back of my hand, that's all."

"He slobbered, trust me... Elle, what is it you have that makes all us men go so silly over you? Three men at one party competing for your attention, you must be able to see it?"

I frowned, "I think you're reading way too much into it. Oscar maybe, mainly because I'm the only girl to have actually dumped him, but Paul Lassiter is just a client, and would only be interested in me to find out why you and Oscar are so fascinated."

"He wants you, I know he wants you, but right now I just want to hold you tight, and kiss you without worrying about smearing your lipstick." He smiled his most dazzling smile, and pulled me onto his lap, leaning in to kiss me softly. As his kisses deepened, they ignited my desire, making me shiver in anticipation of what was to come. I could feel him hardening underneath me, and I slipped my hands under his jacket to feel his warmth radiating through his shirt. I pulled back, and slowly undid his bow tie, leaving the ends dangling around his neck.

Undoing his top button, I gazed at him, "you look very hot like this."

"You looked hot all evening. It took every bit of self control I possess not to book a room, and drag you upstairs," he said, a heated look in his eyes. He pulled me in for another kiss, as we sped through country lanes.

By the time we got back to his, we were both completely turned on, and desperate for some relief. We almost fell into the house, and after a minute greeting the girls, he dragged me upstairs to his bedroom. He made short work of unzipping my dress, and, after I'd stepped out of it, carelessly threw it over a chair, before running his hands over my back to unclip my bra. He quickly shed his jacket, and with slightly trembling fingers, I undid the little buttons of his shirt, before running my hands over his firm muscular chest, trailing my fingers over his tight stomach, and down to the waistband of his trousers. I could see his erection straining, so slipped my hand lower, and lightly caressed it through his clothes. *Whoa that's big Ivan.*

"I have to make you come first Elle, I'm too turned on to last long." He muttered, gently pushing me onto the bed. He shed his clothes in record time, his large erection springing free.

Pressing little kisses up the inside of my thigh, he grasped my knickers and slid them down. With my absence of public hair, I felt exposed and wanton, as he paused a moment to gaze at me, before lightly kissing my clitoris, and burying his nose in me to inhale deeply.

"You smell divine, and you taste like heaven," he whispered in his phone sex voice. I almost came on the spot, especially when he slipped two fingers inside to massage my spot while he lightly sucked my clit. I tried to control the pleasure, but when he started licking my clit with long, soft licks, I had to let go and give in to the orgasm. He lapped and sucked me as I came, groaning with pleasure.

He kissed and licked his way up my body, making me quiver in delight, before finding my nipple, and taking it in his hot, wet mouth, and sucking hard. I felt the sensation travel straight to my groin, causing me to arch off the bed. "You like it hard or gentle?" Ivan murmured against my skin.

"Any way it comes, I like both," I replied, lost in the sensations. My earlier orgasm simply making me even hornier, and desperate to have him inside me. I ogled him shamelessly as he unrolled a condom over himself, his cock was large and thick, but beautiful and smooth, his pubic hair trimmed neatly, but not excessively.

He positioned me on my back, pulling my knees up, and legs apart, and carefully nudged into me, stretching me inside. "You're so tight Elle, feels so good," he panted as he began to move, gently at first, until his thrusts began to speed up, and he began to fuck me at a fast, primal pace, as if he was trying to climb inside me.

I ran my hands over his back, feeling his silky, golden skin, and the hard muscles underneath straining as he hammered into me. Feeling the delicious quivering inside of an impending orgasm, he leaned down to suck my nipple, nipping it gently with his teeth. I fell into my orgasm, it tore through me like a wildfire, scorching me, consuming my entire body. I cried out as I pulsed around him, helpless against the thrusts of his rock hard cock pounding into me, prolonging my climax.

I felt him speed up slightly, before he stilled as he let go, pressing deep into me, his face serene, and slightly vulnerable as he came. Lowering himself onto his elbows, he kissed me. A deep, lush kiss, that conveyed a softness, at odds with the primal, hard fucking I'd just experienced.

He pulled out of me, threw the condom on the bedside cabinet, and lay down beside me, gently running his hands over my tummy in a silky caress. "I've wanted to do that ever since you called me out on those figures at our first meeting, and it was even better than I imagined," he said in his phone sex purr, before pulling me in for another kiss.

The kiss led to another, gentler lovemaking session, Ivan proving to be a sensuous and sensitive lover, frequently changing positions to wring every last drop of pleasure from our connection. He moved slowly, but purposely, timing every thrust perfectly, slowing down every time he felt me on the edge of an orgasm, prolonging the ecstasy. He gazed into my eyes as we both came together, sapphire into light blue, as I clenched and pulsed around him, milking him of everything he had.

We were both panting, and slicked with sweat as he pulled out, leaving me bereft inside. As my heart rate calmed, we both became aware of whimpering and crying outside the bedroom door. "Do you want to let them in?" I asked. He looked amused.

"They'll scratch the door to pieces if I don't. Are you sure you don't mind? They normally sleep in with me, and they're probably confused as to why I shut them out, I just can't do it with them watching."

I giggled, "I wouldn't fancy an audience either, but I'm fine with them on the bed to sleep. Doesn't bother me at all."

"Better get rid of these," he said picking up the condoms, "don't want anyone trying to eat them." He disposed of them in the bathroom before walking over to open the door. I watched with pure feminine appreciation as his muscles flexed sexily when he moved, his skin, flawless and golden. I wondered how I'd won such a prize.

The dogs immediately bounded onto the bed as soon as Ivan opened the door, checking me over, and sniffing me suspiciously. When Ivan got back into bed, they both snuggled up against him possessively.

"Are you being jealous girls," I cooed, rubbing Tania's ears. She pressed herself against Ivan's torso, and closed her eyes firmly.

"I think they're trying to make sure you weren't hurting me," laughed Ivan, looking amused at their antics. He reached over to stroke my face. "You are so very beautiful Elle, and so clever. I can't believe you're finally mine."

I woke up first, and opened my eyes to see Ivan asleep on his back, his arm draped over the pillow, and Bella sprawled out on his chest, snoring softly. Tania was still wedged up against his side, and looked like she hadn't moved all night. I propped myself up on my elbow to see the time on Ivan's bedside clock. It was nearly eight. My movement must have disturbed the dogs, as they both stretched, straining their little legs out, before relaxing back into sleep and snuggles. I slid out of bed, and padded into the bathroom. Looking in the mirror, my beautiful updo resembled a bird's nest, and my perfect makeup was smeared all round my eyes in an imitation of a panda. I quickly washed my face, and took the rubies off, placing them carefully on the surface. It was at that moment, I realised with horror I had no clothes with me, apart from a red ball gown and high heels. I wasn't looking forward to walking in the woods in Jimmy Choos.

I eyed Ivan's toothbrush, and quickly decided we had shared enough germs the previous night to excuse me using it. I brushed my teeth, and headed back to his bedroom. I found my knickers on the floor, and pulled them on, along with Ivan's shirt from the night before. Leaving him sleeping peacefully, I headed downstairs to make a drink.

As I had spent a week staying at Ivan's, I was familiar with his kitchen, and made myself a cup of tea, which I took outside onto the patio to drink. It looked as though it was going to be a beautiful summers day, the sun was already hot for that time of the morning. I sat in a pretty wrought iron chair, and just enjoyed the tranquillity. The only noises were birdsong, and not even a low rumble of traffic in the distance to break the illusion of rural seclusion. I sipped my tea as I replayed the events of the night before in my head. My pride at being introduced as Ivan's girlfriend to his colleagues seemed to merge in my mind with Oscar's sadness that I was on Ivan's arm. I briefly wondered how he knew Dascha.

I smiled as I thought about our passionate lovemaking, glad I had got over my fear of getting naked and physical with Ivan. He had proved to be a great lover, skilful and just the right mixture of gentle and powerful. His body was a work of art, and I shivered at the memory of his thick, silky, cock. All in all, I was a very happy girl.

The arrival of the two spaniels interrupted my reverie, followed by Ivan bearing two coffees. He joined me on the patio, after giving me an extravagant good morning kiss. The dogs raced around the lawn, having sensed it was Sunday, and their play day with Ivan. "And how are you this morning," he asked, settling himself into a chair. He was damp from his shower, and smelt delicious.

"Great, a little bit stiff from all the vigorous activity, but I'm all good," I replied, smiling shyly at him.

"Your hair looks interesting."

"Erm, have you got a brush? I didn't see one in your bathroom. I'm actually a bit stuck for clothes too, so I'll have to nick a t-shirt and some shorts. I don't fancy wearing a ball gown all day."

"Mrs Ballard picked you up a few things, in case you needed them, I think she put them in the spare room you used last time you stayed. Just some clothes, toiletries, that sort of thing."

"Great, thank you for thinking of that." I paused, "so what's the agenda for today?"

"Well, it's Sunday, so either the usual routine of walk, eat and sleep, or anything else you would rather do. I've got nothing planned."

"I can think of something I'd like to do," I flirted, giving him my best sexy smile.

"So can I," he purred, his eyes full of lust, "but I need to feed everyone first, you included, I don't want you passing out on me. You're going to need all your stamina." He winked, making my tummy squeeze with the memory of the pleasure he could inflict. "So, sexy girl, what would you like for breakfast?"

"I'd love a bacon sandwich, I can make it, you sit and have your coffee."

"Nonsense, you're my guest, and I like to cook for you. Why don't you jump in the shower, and I'll have your food ready when you finish?"

"Ok, won't be long." I trotted up the stairs to my old room. To my delight, Jo had stocked the bathroom with my usual shampoo, conditioner and shower gel. I pulled out the grips holding my hair up, and quickly brushed out the tangles before stepping into the shower. Fifteen minutes later, I wrapped myself in a big, fluffy towel, and went to see what was in the walk in wardrobe.

Jo had been extremely practical, and provided shorts, vests, t-shirts, and underwear, as well as a pair of trainers, flip flops, and a bikini. She had clearly taken note of my size when she unpacked my case, as everything looked like it would fit. I pulled on some underwear, shorts and a vest, and slipped on the flip flops.

Back downstairs, Ivan was holding court with the two spaniels, and a plate of sausages. They were gazing adoringly, and wagging their tails so hard, their entire bums were swishing from side to side. "Here, you give them a bit," he said, pushing the plate over to me. I cut off two pieces of sausage, and held them out. As quick as a flash, they were gone, practically inhaled by the eager dogs. They sat looking at me expectantly.

"Am I your new best friend?" I cooed, as I held out more sausage, which they scoffed down straight away, before wagging their tails at me.

"Their affection is so easily bought," said Ivan, grinning at them, and grabbing a sandwich.

Chapter 5

It was wonderfully cool in the woods, the trees providing a dappled shade, as we wandered through, holding hands. I had discovered that Ivan was extremely tactile, wanting to be in bodily contact with me all the time, either stroking my arm, touching my face, or keeping my hand in his. The girls raced around at our feet, as we walked in companionable silence. I begun to relax, feeling the tension leaving my hands and shoulders. "No regrets?" Ivan asked. I gave him a quizzical look. "About us," he said.

"None at all. Why, have you?"

"No, of course not. I wanted you from the moment I saw you. I'm just relieved we finally got together. I was worried that Oscar would claim you as his."

I laughed, "I was told you only dated supermodels, so I didn't think you'd be interested in a little swot like me. Plus I thought I'd upset you by challenging you in that first meeting."

"You didn't upset me, I was impressed, and intrigued. I knew from that moment that I had to get to know you."

An hour later, we got back to the house. The sun had begun to blaze, so we decided to swim before lunch. I went upstairs to change into the bikini Jo had thoughtfully provided. As I walked into the bedroom, I heard my phone buzzing in my clutch. I pulled it out, but it had rung off. Frowning, I noticed I had 22 missed calls from my mum. I called her back straightaway.

Ray answered, "Elle, I've been trying to get hold of you all morning. It's your mum," he paused, "I found her dead this morning." His voice cracked, "I'm so very sorry."

I went cold, my spine prickling, "What? How? What happened?" I was struggling to get the words out. I sat down on the edge of the bed.

"We don't know yet, but the early indications are that she had a brain aneurysm. I think she got up in the night, I found her in the hall." He let out a sob. "I called an ambulance right away, but the paramedics said she had been dead several hours....Elle, I don't know what to do."

"Where are you?"

"At the flat. They took her away in the ambulance. They're going to want to do a post mortem, and the police need to come and interview me, as it was a sudden death."

"When did all this happen?"

"I found her about an hour ago. We had a late night last night, didn't get home till nearly two, so I had a lay in."

"Ray, I'm on my way. I'm coming from Sussex, but I'll be as quick as I can. Stay there."

"Will do, and Elle,"

"Yeah?"

"I loved her too."

"I know." I rang off, and sat for a moment, reeling from the shock. Ivan wandered in to see what was keeping me. One look at my face wiped the smile off of his. "My mum's been found dead. I need Roger to drive me to Welling, if that's ok."

He wrapped his arms around me, and said; "Baby I'm so sorry, whatever you need. I'll call Roger. I'll come with you."

The dam burst, and I sobbed into his chest. He held me with one strong arm, while he pulled his phone out of his pocket with the other, and called for Roger to bring the car round, and someone to take care of the dogs. He sat me down on the bed while he threw on a T-shirt, and some shoes, and gathered up my house keys and mobile, before leading me out to the car.

He let me cry into his chest, and simply sat stroking my hair, and passing me tissues. He felt solid and steadfast, a strong man who didn't shirk away from emotional difficulties as well as practical ones. We sped along the M25 towards the place I had tried to airbrush from my life, but needed now that it was gone. Roger negotiated the traffic like the professional he was, and before I knew it, we were pulling into Lovell Avenue.

I cringed slightly as the Bentley pulled up outside the tiny maisonettes, and parked alongside the elderly Fiats and Fords. I had hoped Ivan would never see where I came from, but at that moment, I just wanted to be inside my childhood home. The police were already there, in the living room, sitting with Ray, asking about timings and circumstances. The neighbour from downstairs had been making everyone cups of tea, and no doubt earwigging. A death in the estate was big news that would keep the gossips occupied for weeks.

"That was quick," said Ray, pulling me into a hug, "officers, this is Elle Reynolds, Debbie's daughter." The officers stood, and offered their condolences. I sat down on the scruffy velour sofa, and listened to the rest of the interview. Ivan disappeared into the kitchen.

It seemed that mum and Ray had been to a 'do' the night before. Both had been drinking and dancing, although Ray said neither were terribly drunk. They had got home around half one, had toast and a cup of tea, and gone to bed. He had woken up at ten, got up, and discovered her on the floor in the hall. At first, he'd assumed she'd fainted, so had wrapped a blanket round her while he waited for the ambulance. They arrived within fifteen minutes, and told him she'd been dead for several hours. The police made notes as he spoke, raising no concerns of foul play. To be fair, Ray looked shell shocked, and kept breaking down into sobs. The police took my details too, before again, murmuring their condolences, and promising to be in touch once the cause of death had been ascertained.

Ivan came out of the kitchen bearing mugs of tea. It shamed me to see that every mug was chipped, but he didn't seem to care. "I heard what happened," he said, "I was listening. Do you know when they'll find out what the post mortem says?"

"A few days I think," replied Ray, sipping his tea gratefully. I sat quietly and looked around the tiny living room, with it's cheap ornaments and scruffy wallpaper, committing it all to memory. Despite feeling shamed by it, it was still home, with its familiar, and comforting smell. I noticed mum had framed a snapshot of me at my graduation from Cambridge, I was wearing my mortarboard and gown, smiling proudly. I remembered that moment well, it had felt like my first steps to freedom. I glanced at Ivan, who's eyes had alighted on the photo as well.

"She was very proud of you," he stated.

"Used to boast about Elle to everyone. Said she was the brains of the family," said Ray.

Family. I have no family now. Nobody at all. The thought hit me like a sledgehammer. I think Ivan sensed that I was melting down slightly. He wrapped an arm around my shoulder, and squeezed me tight. I was grateful to him for being there. I also felt slightly sorry for him that his day of wild sex had ended up being a day sitting in a grotty flat in suburbia with a snotty, and tearful girlfriend. "I'm sorry, this wasn't how today was meant to pan out," I said to Ivan. He just hugged me tighter.

"What kind of man would I be if I was only with you on the good days?" Ivan replied. I sniffed.

"Elle, there's something I need to ask you, I know it's not a good time, but what are you going to do with the flat?" Ray asked, "only I gave up my digs to move in with your mum. I don't have anywhere else to go if you want to move back and take over the tenancy."

"I don't want to move back here Ray. You have it. I'll just want a few personal things, photos, that's all. You keep the furniture and stuff." He looked relieved. I went to the drawer in the dresser where mum kept all the photos, and pulled them out, there weren't many, but developing film had been expensive in the days before digital cameras. Ray went to the kitchen to pull a Lidl bag out of a cupboard for me to carry the albums. I went to her bedroom, and stared at the familiar old dressing table that she'd found in a junk shop in Plumstead. I knew she'd sold every scrap of jewellery she'd possessed to buy my books for university, so I silently said goodbye to her empty bed, and closed the door.

I promised Ray that I would register the death, and organise the funeral as soon as the police or coroner gave me the go ahead. I took one last look around the flat, silently saying goodbye to the ghost of my mother, and the girl I used to be, and I walked outside with Ivan, gripping his hand tightly.

"Can you take me back to London please?" I said. I needed to be alone. All I wanted to do was curl up and cry, without worrying about how I looked, or how he was feeling.

"Are you sure? I don't mind where we go, but it might be better to have the tranquillity of the estate if you need to grieve."

I smiled gratefully, "you're wonderful, did you know that? But I need to be alone right now." He nodded, and spoke to Roger. We pulled away, and headed towards London.

He hovered around when we got back to the flat, sending a member of security out for groceries. He had placed the bag of photos on the kitchen island, an innocuous bag that I was afraid to open.

"Tell me about your mother, what sort of person was she?" Ivan asked.

I thought for a moment, "she was fun, had a great sense of humour. Liked music, drinking and the soaps. Made a lot of poor choices in life, narrow outlook. That's it really."

"She made you, so she must have been quite something," he said softly.

"I was ashamed of it, of taking you there. Seeing the cheap, scruffy place I come from. Seeing you drink from a chipped mug. I wanted to hide it from you. I escaped that life." My tears started to fall again. Ivan, to his credit, wrapped his strong arms around me, and kissed my wet face.

"It's a palace compared to what I grew up in. Your mother did her best for you. Never forget that. She loved you. Be proud of who you are, and where your journey began."

"It's all gone now. Nothing to run away from," I sniffed in a very unladylike way, "I have no family at all now. Nobody, not even a cousin." Ivan pulled a square of kitchen roll off, and handed it to me so I could blow my nose. I noticed I'd left a wet patch on his T-shirt, and hoped it wasn't snot.

"I know how that feels, and believe me when I say you'll survive it. She gave you brains and self reliance. That's a great legacy. Plus you have a knack of pulling rich men," he smiled as I laughed, albeit a rather half hearted one. He was right, I could take care of myself just fine.

I missed Ivan almost the moment he left. He hadn't wanted to go, but I'd insisted I needed time alone. I poured myself a large glass of wine, and called James.

"Hey, little Elle, how's things?"

"Bad, really bad." I sniffed. "My mum died this morning." Just saying the words squeezed teardrops out of my eyes.

"Oh Elle, you poor girl. What happened?" James sounded so sympathetic, it squeezed more tears out.

"Brain haemorrhage. Her partner found her dead on the floor this morning."

"That must have been a hell of a shock for both of you. Had she been ill?"

"No, it came out of the blue. Ray's in shock."

"You sound as though you are too Elle. Is there anyone who can come round and sit with you?"

"No. Ivan was with me earlier, but I sent him home. I wanted to be alone. I've done nothing but cry all day."

"That's normal. Losing a parent is harder than people realise. It hits everyone in different ways. Being tearful is to be expected. Don't be so hard on yourself Elle, if you need to cry, then just let it out. Anyone who's lost a parent will understand. All of us cry when our mums die, even us big, hairy blokes." I stayed silent, just listening to James' soothing voice, and I wished he wasn't in America.

After our call, I wandered to the island, and pulled the albums out of the bag. They were cheap, plastic affairs, no doubt from Wilkinsons. I opened the first one to see a picture of myself age about three, sitting on a swing, hanging on for grim death. I flicked through the albums, smiling at some of the memories, cringing at some others.

I was interrupted by a knock on the door. Assuming it was Ivan, I opened it straightaway, only to find Oscar standing there, looking a bit sheepish. I stood aside to let him in, and he frowned when he saw my puffy, tear stained face. "What can I do for you?" I asked.

"I came to apologise for last night," he paused, "Elle, have you been crying?"

"Yeah, I had some bad news today, nothing for you to worry about though." I didn't want to say the words or tell the story again, and certainly not to Oscar. "Don't concern yourself with last night, I'm over it. Can you muzzle your girlfriend if I have to run into her again though please."

"She's not my girlfriend. I don't know why she said that."

"I do, and it really doesn't matter Oscar."

"You looked beautiful. I could barely take my eyes off you. I wanted to tell you."

I sighed, "it was just a pretty dress and a pair of shoes Oscar, it was still just me underneath. Your date was stunning. She might have been a bitch, but at least she was a pretty one."

He scowled. "I didn't appreciate her comments about you. I won't be seeing her again..... Did Ivan make you cry?"

"No, of course not. Don't be silly."

"Well what then? Dammit Elle, you look like you've been crying all day, will you just tell me what's wrong?"

"There's no need to shout at me. It's nothing that concerns you, Ivan or anyone else for that matter, so I'd appreciate it if you stopped jumping to conclusions." A thick silence spread between us. Oscar wasn't budging. "My mum was found dead this morning. They think it was a brain haemorrhage."

He stared at me for a moment, before pulling me into his arms, and enveloping me in a hug. "Elle, I'm so sorry for you."

"Oscar, please, I'll end up crying again, and my eyes are sore."

"Why are you here on your own?"

"I wanted to be alone. I need to sit quietly and think. Today has been overwhelming in lots of ways," I breathed in Oscar's lovely Oscary smell before pulling away, "I had to go home, only I didn't want it to be home, and there was nothing for me to bring back here apart from a couple of photos, and that made me so sad for her......I'm not making sense am I?"

"Nothing to remember her by? At all?"

"Nope. She sold all her jewellery to help me buy books for uni. She had nothing Oscar. I feel so bloody guilty about that. Dascha was right on Saturday night, Ivan bought my outfit, and the rubies I was wearing. I was nothing but a fraud, parading round like I belonged. The truth is that I'm living a life that isn't mine, and it hurts to know that she died never having had anything nice in her life." The blasted tears began leaking out again, and I grabbed another bit of kitchen roll to blow my nose. *Yeah, alright Oscar, I'm no lady.*

"Your mum had you. Far more precious than a bit of stone. I know which I'd choose if I had to make a choice. Elle, it doesn't matter if someone else chose that dress, you looked beautiful in it, and that's all that matters. Don't ever forget that twenty thousand pounds to Ivan is like twenty pence to someone like your mother, so to him it was just a nice little treat for you, and certainly nothing to feel guilty about. As for Dascha, I gather she spent his money like water when she had the chance. He told me once that she spent half a million on one shopping trip alone, so I don't think she's got any right to sneer at you."

I sniffed in a very unladylike way. "I know it shouldn't have rattled me, but it did. Now, I appreciate your apology for her behaviour, I really do, but right now I need to be alone. I hope you understand."

"Of course. I'll leave you to it. I'm just downstairs if you need anything. I mean it, anything you need, just call or knock." He gave me a small smile, and a slightly awkward hug, before leaving.

I made myself a coffee, and sat at the island. It was only six o'clock, so I pulled out my laptop, and tried to lose myself in the work I had to catch up on. By eight, I was finished, and pacing around the flat, not wanting to watch telly, listen to music, or any other activity. My phone sat on the island, and I scrolled through the texts from my mum, the final one being sent the first Sunday I spent with Ivan.

I almost dropped the damn thing when it made me jump by starting to ring. I answered straightaway, "hi Ivan."

"How are you?"

"Ok. Bored, trying not to think too much. You?"

"Bored, the girls are asleep. There's nothing on telly."

"Can I come over?"

"I'll send a car." He cut the call. *I really need to talk to him about that.*

Approximately ten minutes later, I was in the Bentley, heading to Saffron Wharf, and the strongest man I'd ever met. I was escorted up to the apartment by Roger, and almost fell into Ivan's waiting arms. He kissed me softly and sweetly, and sat me on the sofa in the lounge while he poured us each a glass of wine.

We snuggled on the sofa all the evening, Ivan kept an arm around me, holding me firm. We didn't discuss the events of the day, keeping our conversations lighter, mainly about the girls, and their dreadful behaviour at times. By ten, I was fast asleep.

Ivan must have carried me to bed. I woke up at half five, wearing just my bra and knickers, with Ivan and the girls fast asleep in a big sleep heap beside me. I tried to slip out of bed without waking him, but as soon as my foot touched the floor, he opened his eyes. "God, you get up early. Are you staying for breakfast, or do you need to go straight home?"

"I need to go home and start getting ready."

"Just dial 1 on the phone over there, and they'll send a car for you."

"Ok. Thanks." I padded around to the other side of the bed, and leaned down to give Ivan a soft kiss. I called down to the security team before pulling on my shorts and vest from the previous day, and slipping on the flip flops. Ivan had gone back to sleep, so I slipped away, and went downstairs to wait for my car.

The first thing I did when I got into work was to go and see Lewis to tell him what had happened, and to let him know that I'd need to take time off at some point for the funeral and the administrative details. He was full of sympathy, and asked if I needed compassionate leave, which I declined. The idea of sitting alone in my flat doing nothing filled me with horror. I was better off losing myself in work, and was actually looking forward to concentrating on a detailed contract, as it would take my mind off the overwhelming guilt I was feeling. Thankfully, the morning passed in a blur of emails, calls and paperwork. Ivan had sent me an email asking if I was ok, and enquiring how my day was going. I'd replied that I was keeping busy, and was coping fine.

I had no lunch meeting planned, so at twelve, I went to see if Priti wanted to join me for a sandwich. We headed down to her favourite cafe, waving at Giuseppe as we walked past the salon. "Who's that?" She asked.

"He did my hair Saturday for a ball. Put it up in a sort of chignon. Did an amazing job, so I think I'm gonna make him my regular hairdresser."

"I might give him a try. I saw your hair on the Citigossip website. You looked amazing......." Priti paused, "and so did Ivan. You realise I need to know every detail."

"I'm not spilling every detail, some details can't be shared you know. Call it client confidentiality."

She snorted with laughter. "There are certain details you're compelled to share, and I don't mean anything about his legal affairs."

"I know exactly what you're on about, and I suggest you keep dreaming. I didn't realise there would be pictures online. There were photographers there, but there were quite a few famous people attending, so I didn't think they'd be interested in me."

"I saw loads of pictures," said Priti, "and people asking who the lady in red was. Ivan's quite the celeb in business circles."

"Hopefully they won't find out who I am, and move on to someone more interesting." We chose our lunches and sat down. I told her about Oscar's date, the insult, and the actor I had been seated next to, who was a favourite of hers. By the time we had finished lunch, Priti had enough of a gossip fix to stop her asking tricky questions about Ivan. It also stopped me having to tell her about mum.

I walked back into my office to find a beautiful arrangement of calla lilies. I opened the card, and read a sweet message of condolence from Oscar. I pulled my mobile out of my bag, and sent a text thanking him. I decided to keep the flowers in the office as they looked rather stylish, and took a little of the bareness away.

The afternoon seemed a little quiet. I suspected that Lewis had asked my colleagues not to lumber me with too much work, or bother me with lots of calls. I didn't even have any client meetings until the next day, when I was accompanying the publisher to her negotiations. As I had no idea what type of contract she would need, I couldn't even do any preparation. For the first time since I'd worked at Pearson Hardwick, I was kicking my heels. I went to see Lewis to find out if there was anything I could help with. He shook his head and waved me out, telling me to take the afternoon off. Normally I would have bitten his hand off, but I didn't want to go home and sit in an empty flat. I called Ivan to see what he was up to.

"Hi baby, you ok?" Ivan asked when he picked up.

"Yeah, I'm ok. Bit bored, have you got anything for me?"

"Not today, no. Listen, I'm a bit tied up right now, can I call you back later?"

"Of course. Speak to you later."

Ivan cut the call, *without saying goodbye grrr.*

Chapter 6

In the absence of anything meaningful to do, I did what every self respecting girl-about-town would do, I went shopping. I didn't really look at clothes, as I had plenty to be going on with, but I treated myself to some new makeup, new lingerie, and some expensive face cream. I spent a nice hour perusing the perfume counter in Jo Malone, where I decided I liked Black Pomegranate, and visited hotel chocolat to try and acquire a taste for poncey chocolate.

I ended up in Waterstones, where I scanned the self help books, trying to find one on dealing with guilt, and low self esteem. I was flicking through one, when I was interrupted by a voice whispering behind me. "Have you found what you're looking for?"

I spun round, and came face to face with Paul Lassiter. "You made me jump," I gasped, "creeping up on me like that."

"You were in a world of your own," he said, taking the book out of my hands and reading the title. He frowned, "raise your own self esteem? Why are you looking at this?" I snatched back the book, and replaced it on the shelf.

"Just looking," I replied, "what are you in here for?"

"The new Jeffrey Archer. I'm a big fan."

"Oh, is it out? I love his books. I read the first two in the trilogy. I might get it as well, it'll give me something to do tonight." Losing myself in a good book wasn't a bad idea.

"Not seeing Ivan tonight?" Paul asked. He seemed to have a distinctly non-predatory way about him, unlike the two men I'd been dealing with recently.

"Don't think so. He was busy earlier." We found the stack of Jeffrey Archer's latest novel, and both headed to the checkout.

"Would you like a coffee, we can discuss our favourite books," he said, giving me his boyish smile.

"Ok, won't be a minute," I said, before paying at the checkout. He waited for me, then led me over to the costa at the back of the shop, finding two comfy sofas for us. I sat down with all my bags, while he got our coffees.

I watched him at the counter, noting that his suit wasn't bespoke, and his shoes weren't handmade. Somehow it made him more approachable and human, a trait I couldn't attribute to either Ivan or Oscar, both of whom took immaculate dressing to new heights.

He placed a large mug of latte on the low table in front of me, and sat down on the sofa opposite. There weren't many people in the cafe, so I didn't feel guilty about hogging the two sofas.

"Who were you there with on Saturday? I don't think I was introduced to your girlfriend," I said, blowing the steam off my coffee.

"I took my sister, only she ditched me at the first opportunity to chat up some rugby player," he replied, pulling a face. "You looked nice, although I couldn't help but notice that you didn't look too happy." *Nice? Don't strain yourself with the compliments Paul.*

"Oscar's date was a bit snippy with me. I gather she was Ivan's ex."

"And didn't take kindly to both men falling at your feet?"

"They're not falling at anyone's feet. Ivan took me as a colleague, he thought it would be a great networking opportunity for me, which it was."

"Ivan kept his arm clamped round your waist the whole time, and Golding was practically prostrate at your feet. Couldn't take his sad little eyes off you. Everyone saw it. I thought it was quite funny, although I did think Ivan was gonna punch me when I kissed your hand."

I laughed, "I doubt it, although I wouldn't put it past his bodyguards, they seem to be as possessive as Ivan."

"You're a real conundrum Elle. I can't work you out at all. For someone so self contained and cool, some bitch who's one step up from a hooker managed to rattle you at that ball. You were on the arm of a wealthy, handsome man, yet you looked really uncomfortable.... Am I wrong?"

"I'm not uncomfortable with Ivan at all, I was rattled by the snide comments she made, that was all. She just pressed the right buttons."

"You looked slightly awkward. I know he calls you his girlfriend, but your body language said different."

"Are you an expert in body language?" I was genuinely interested. Paul was proving to be a rather perceptive man.

"Yes. I studied the subject a lot. I have to be able to read people quickly. I am a headhunter by trade you know."

"Ok Paul, how did you read the situation on Saturday?" He looked thoughtful for a moment, as if he was measuring his words.

"This is between the two of us?" I nodded. "I think Oscar is in love with you, but is too emotionally stunted to know how to handle it, and I think Ivan wishes to possess you, in the same way that he wants to own the world. He views you as a grand prize, knowing that Oscar, who has the one thing that Ivan cannot have, which is breeding, views you as his perfect woman."

"I see. That's rather a low view of Ivan isn't it? He actually made a play for me around the same time I began seeing Oscar. Personally I can't see why either of them find me so fascinating. I'm very ordinary, and both of them could do better."

Paul smiled, "and now I know why you were looking at that book. It makes sense now. It also tells me why you looked so uncomfortable over that woman's comments."

"Do tell," I said, keeping my face impassive. *Who does he think he is?*

"Did she make a comment about Ivan buying you your outfit?" *Ok, so you're good at this.*

"Yes, that came into it."

"And it made you uncomfortable because you're a clever, independent woman, who earns like a man in your world?" I nodded, not wanting to speak. I didn't want to confirm or deny his assessment. "In their world, you're just a nice girl to be looked after, treated to pretty things, and taken care of. Yet you didn't struggle through years of law school to be no different from a pretty airhead did you? It rubs against your grain, diminishes your achievements, so consciously or subconsciously, you find it a problem."

"All very perceptive Paul. So what's your ulterior motive?"

"Me? I just think you've got a cracking pair of tits, but I'm a simple man with simple tastes."

I laughed, "I suppose at least you're honest, but quite frankly Paul, despite your detailed analysis, I have to work for all three of you, so it has to be professional all the way. Now, changing the subject, can you recommend any good books on reading too much into people's body language?"

Paul laughed, "I certainly can. I think I've read every book that exists on the subject. I can email you the Amazon links if you like. Some of the better ones are too obscure for a bookshop."

"That would be great thanks. By the way, I should have the new company numbers, and Articles of Associations for your new companies by the end of the week. You can begin trading under them right away, but I'd recommend you wait till your new bank accounts and insurance details are changed over first."

"That's fantastic news. Should save me a few quid in tax. I already sorted the new accounts with Goldings, so I can change my indemnities to Monday, and begin. You never know Elle, cut my tax bill enough, and I too might be able to afford an expensive girlfriend."

I frowned, "I'm sure you're not short of thruppence. Can I ask though, why did you take your sister on Saturday, and not a date?"

He smiled, "oh I don't date, not in the traditional sense anyway."

"Really? Why's that?"

"I hate the superficiality of the dating thing. I can't bear a whole evening spent with a dozy airhead who wants to discuss Brangelina and shopping, so I don't do it. I prefer to be alone." *Weirdo alert.*

"That's interesting, anyway Paul, thanks for the coffee. I'm going to head home and make a start on Jeffrey." I stood and gathered my bags.

"Yes, me too. Well it's been lovely to see you again, and I'll email you about the books." He kissed my cheek, and I headed out.

It had been a strange conversation, and I was a touch unnerved by it. On the surface, he had pleaded almost poverty, yet I knew he was extremely wealthy, and the whole 'not dating' thing was really weird. As I perused the ready meals in the deli, I wondered if he was one of those odd dominants like the one portrayed in fifty shades. Either way, I would be keeping my distance.

I lugged all my bags home, mildly disappointed that Roger obviously hadn't been on phone tracking duties that afternoon. Back at the flat, I unpacked everything, adding my new lingerie to the now slightly fuller closet, and made a nice coffee to go with my novel. At least it had taken my mind off events for a few hours, although I had the whole evening to get through without becoming maudlin yet.

I had barely read the first chapter when my phone rang with an unknown number. I answered it, expecting it to be the police or coroner. "Hello Elle, hope you don't mind me calling," said Lady Golding, "but Oscar told me about your poor mother. I just wanted to offer my condolences."

"That's very kind of you Lady Golding, thank you. Oscar did send some lovely flowers."

"Good. I also heard that his dreadful date on Saturday night insulted you. Some of these girls just have no manners at all."

"I agree, mind you, with the events of Sunday, I really have forgotten all about it. None of it seems so important now. By the way, how's Mrs Smith?"

"I haven't really spoken to her much. She's been disgraced by the whole sorry saga. Her husband left her as well. I gather she was stealing the money for her lover, not herself as such, so her husband found out about her affair, although she claimed it had ended years ago."

"That's rather curious isn't it? That she would steal money for someone she had a fling with years back. Why would anyone do that?"

Lady Golding sighed, "I think she still held a torch for him, hoped he'd return to her. She was just a silly old woman really. She refuses to tell anyone how much she took though."

"It was a hell of a lot, Lady Golding. Nearly bankrupted the factory. That factory is a big employer in the area, a lot of family breadwinners depend on it. If people knew how close they took it to closure, well, she wouldn't be popular."

"Dreadful business. It was jolly lucky you stepped in when you did, is all I can say. Did Oscar tell you that the church newsletter went down a storm? Lots of people have commented on how wonderful it was. Oscar has suggested that I go on a computer course to learn how to do it the way that you did."

"Sounds like a great idea. Personally, I think you should write a book about Conniscliffe's previous occupants. You tell such brilliant stories about them. I'd read it. If you didn't want to type it all, you could always get an assistant. That's what Dame Barbara Cartland used to do. She just dictated her stories, and the assistant typed them up."

"Really? What a nice idea. I think I'll put that to Oscar. It's been lovely to speak to you again Elle, and once again, I'm sorry about your bad news."

"Thank you, and thanks for calling." We said our goodbyes, and ended the call. I had just got back into my book when it rang again. "Hi Ivan."

"Hi baby, you home from work yet?"

"Yes. I had nothing much on this afternoon, so Lewis sent me home. I went shopping instead."

"Without me?"

"Yes," I replied, as if talking to a child, "I only bought a book, some makeup, perfume, that type of thing. I'm perfectly capable of shopping alone you know. Anyway, you were busy."

"I would have sent Roger over with a credit card." He sounded sulky.

"Don't be silly, I don't need that, I didn't buy that much, and besides, I just got paid." I didn't have to send money to my mum anymore either, but I kept quiet about that.

"I like treating you. I want you to have the best of everything. I don't know why you are so resistant to that."

I thought about my conversation with Paul. "I appreciate the things you give me, but I also appreciate the things I work hard for. Allow me to have that, please."

"Hmm. So what are you up to tonight? Would you like to go out to dinner?"

I thought about the tragic little lasagne in the fridge, waiting to be heated up, and replied, "that sounds lovely. Where shall we go?"

"Why don't you call your new concierge service that I bought for you today, and get them to book somewhere nice? I emailed you the details. I'll pick you up at half seven. Is that ok?"

I opened my laptop, and found the email. "Ivan, that's brilliant. I'll give them a call. See you in a bit."

Quintessentially yours proved to be extremely knowledgeable regarding restaurants, and quickly booked me a table at Quaglinos, before emailing me a confirmation and directions. *How useful is that?* I quickly showered, and pulled on my new black lace bra and thong set, before choosing one of my new dresses to wear.

Thankfully, my legs were still brown from my application of St Tropez on Saturday, so I didn't have to bother with tights. I looked in the mirror to check my appearance. I looked expensively stylish in the dress, but still sad around the eyes. I added a touch more mascara, and grabbed my handbag as the buzzer sounded to let me know that the car was downstairs.

Quaglinos was delightful. Ivan was pleased that his security could be seated at the huge bar, just a few steps away, and we both loved the food. He told me about his day, which had sounded quite tedious, concerned mainly with admin details and staffing issues, and I told him about my shopping trip. I decided it was best to tell him I bumped into Paul Lassiter, as I had nothing to hide, and Paul was a client.

"He took his sister Saturday night. Said he doesn't date, which is odd isn't it?"

"He's a rather strange man. Pleads poverty the whole time, but he's filthy rich." Ivan said.

"Are you sure? He doesn't look it, or sound it. His office is very basic too."

"Yes, I'm sure. I think he just doesn't like to spend it. Did he make a move on you?"

"No," I shook my head, "he's friendly, but not overly enamoured I don't think. I got the impression that he has issues with women, although I'm not sure why."

"You think he's gay?"

"No, not gay, just, oh I don't know, like one of those men who likes to have contractual sex relationships only. That sort of thing. Don't worry, he didn't proposition me."

Ivan laughed, "I'm sure he values his testicles too much to ask you to become his sex slave. I, on the other hand, am a reckless man, with a security team two steps away." He smiled his dazzling smile at me, which made me laugh.

"You want me to be your sex slave?"

"It would fulfil every adolescent sex fantasy I ever wanked to. So yes, I would dearly love to make you my slave."

"I'd have to see the job description first," I flirted.

"It would involve taking every bit of pleasure I could possibly throw at you, orgasming frequently, and allowing me carte Blanche to fuck you in every way known to man." Ivan was using his phone sex voice. My belly squeezed. "I would begin with a quick fuck in the car on the way home, then I'd tie you to my sex swing, and fuck you nonstop for three orgasms."

"Get the bill." I replied, feeling hot and flustered. Ivan gestured to the waiter to bring the bill.

"Go to the ladies, and take your knickers off. Put them in your handbag, and come out with your pussy bare," he purred, "I'll meet you back here." I did as he asked, tucking the tiny triangle of lace into my bag. I rejoined him at the table.

"Now, give me your knickers please," Ivan said. I handed him the tiny folded triangle with a puzzled look. He held them to his face, and inhaled before tucking them in his pocket. I glanced around in panic to see if anyone was watching, but people seemed to be focused on their food, and their own companions. Ivan's eyes glittered as he watched me, amused at my horrified look. "You smell so good, I can't wait to eat you."

"You are so....naughty at times," I admonished him, "what if someone saw that?"

"Oh, that's half the fun. Now, shall we go?"

I had to walk the whole length of the restaurant with Ivan's hand against the small of my back, which was heating up rapidly. My clitoris began to pulse as the knowledge of what was to come caused it to swell and twitch. I had to stop myself dragging Ivan out of the door when he stopped to chat to someone he knew, my frustration building with every passing moment. After a few minutes of business talk, he gave me an amused look, before telling his acquaintance that we had better be going. I was relieved, as by then my nipples were like bullets, and my legs were getting a bit wobbly.

As soon as we were in the car, he slid the privacy screen up, and undid his trousers to reveal a solid erection, reined in by his tight jersey boxers. I was so horny by then, I could have happily ripped them off with my teeth. He quickly unrolled a condom over himself, and pulled me to straddle him, making me pause slightly for him to stare at me with my dress around my waist, before impaling me on his large dick.

I rode him hard, revelling in the feel of his large cock repeatedly hitting my g spot. I grasped the headrest to allow myself to lean back slightly and change the angle of my ascent, increasing the pressure on the deepest, most sensitive part of me. I carried on riding him right through my orgasm, which seemed to make it go on and on, until his hands pulled my hips down and held them still, as he tipped over the edge himself.

I watched him come, his beautiful face tightened into a slight scowl, before softening as he let go. I caught a moment of vulnerability, but it was fleeting, replaced by a smile, and a soft kiss.

"You can stop driving now," Ivan said into the intercom. I blushed. I hadn't realised we'd been driving around the block. I lifted myself off him, and smoothed my dress down, as he wrapped the condom in a napkin, and tucked himself back into his trousers.

He practically dragged me into the flat, before kissing me deeply inside the front hall, while the girls tapped and pawed at him for attention. "Not now girls, go play with your toys," he muttered, before leading me upstairs. "Do you trust me enough to be my sex slave tonight?"

I nodded, my earlier orgasm had only served to whet my appetite. I had an almost unbearable tension building inside me, that I needed him to release. I expected him to lead me to his bedroom, but he surprised me by taking me to one of the spare rooms further down the hall, which I hadn't been in before. He pulled me in, and closed the door, before switching the light on.

The room was large, fairly bare, save for an enormous bed against the centre of the right hand wall, a swing suspended from the ceiling, and a large cabinet against the right hand wall. "This, my darling, is my pleasure room, and you are cordially invited to join me here tonight." He grasped my hand, and led me into the room, before stopping and giving me a deep, lush kiss, his hands holding the sides of my head, keeping me still. He pulled back, and gazed into my eyes, as if seeking permission. I smiled, and kissed him back, my hands running over his chest, and over his abs, till I reached his waistband. "Let me get you naked, and help you into the swing," he said, "nothing will hurt, I promise. This is all for pleasure." He unzipped my dress, and peeled it off my shoulders, letting it drop to the floor. I stepped out of it, and stood in just my shoes and bra. He reached round and unclasped it, letting it drop on top of my dress. He ran his hands reverently over my breasts, lingering on my peaked nipples, before dipping down to take one in his mouth, and sucking hard. I cried out, arching my back to release the exquisite pressure of his mouth on my breast. I had a brief respite while he moved to give the other nipple the same attention. His hand slid between my legs, and he murmured, "you're soaked, I really like that. I can't wait to taste it. Come, let's get you into the swing."

At first glance, it looked like an impossibly complex contraption, but Ivan showed me where to sit, and lay back into the sling. Even with the stirrups cuffed around my ankles, it was surprisingly comfortable. Ivan cuffed my wrists to the swing, around my ears, using soft leather shackles, and there I lay, fully exposed, and totally helpless.

Ivan began to slowly undress, almost teasing me, all the time watching my reactions, and gazing at my exposed body. "You look so lovely like that darling, every bit of you is mine tonight, and I'm going to give you the best fuck of your life." I almost came there and then. When he was naked, he wandered over to the cabinet, and opened one side to reveal an iPod player. He pressed a button on the remote, and a techno beat, with a deep base began to play. He picked up another remote and pointed it at the ceiling. I felt my legs begin to rise, followed by my body. When I was at his shoulder level, with my legs pulled up, and apart, he stopped the device. I was totally exposed to him, and at his mercy.

He gently stroked my inner thighs, running his index fingers up and down, igniting tiny trails with just his touch. He began to press tiny kisses where his fingers had been, before pressing a featherlight kiss on my clitoris. I convulsed at the contact. He grasped my thighs to keep the swing still, and began with the softest, lightest licks, lapping at me, tasting my arousal, before lightly sucking in my clit. I cried out. With everything held immobile, I seemed to have no way of controlling my pleasure, I couldn't close my legs, or move in any way. I just had to give in, and come hard, all over his face. He lapped as I pulsed and clenched with my orgasm, before finally coming up for air.

I could see his face glistening wet in the low light, and he wiped it with his hand, before using the remote to lower the swing to hip height. At the cabinet, he slid on a condom, before grabbing a vibrator, and thrusting his huge cock straight into me. Using the motion of the swing, he slammed into me again and again, fucking me without mercy, pulling right out to the tip, before slamming back in, all the way to the root. The wide crest of his cock was bumping repeatedly over my g spot, building a huge deep orgasm inside, which threatened to tear me apart.

With one hand gripping my thighs, keeping the rhythm going, he clicked the vibrator on with the other, and pressed it against my clit while he carried on pounding me. I tried to absorb the pleasure, but it rapidly pushed me over the edge, and I detonated with a scream, pulsing helplessly around his huge cock, and not wanting the torture to end. My orgasm didn't even subside. As Ivan continued to hammer into me, I came again and again, till they were just rolling through me. My entire body was shaking uncontrollably, and all I could do was give myself over to the intense sensations.

Ivan came with a shout. He was dripping with sweat, as he pressed into me, stilling as he poured himself inside me. I could feel his cock twitching and jerking, as he shuddered with the aftershocks. He smiled a triumphant smile before pulling out, quickly releasing me from the shackles, and helping me down.

We both staggered bonelessly over to the large bed, flopping down side by side. "That was amazing," I said, "I didn't even know my body was capable of that many orgasms."

"What's your name?" Ivan asked.

"Can't remember," I replied.

Chapter 7

I woke early the next morning, and stretched my aching body, feeling as stiff as a board, and completely wrung out. Nicking a bathrobe from the back of the bathroom door, I headed down to the kitchen for a cup of tea. Neither Ivan, nor either of the dogs even stirred. I decided to forego the gym, and go straight to my meeting at The Strand, where I'd be sitting in on a negotiation for the acquisition of a publishing company. I had to be there at nine thirty, so it would be quite a leisurely morning. I calculated that I needed to be home by half seven to get ready, so had plenty of time to relax. I took my tea out to the terrace, and sat watching the boats chugging past.

Ivan and the dogs appeared about half an hour later, the dogs racing down to the far end of the terrace, where Ivan explained, there was a square of grass planted, which acted as a sort of indoor/outdoor loo for them. He laughed when I wrinkled my nose, explaining it was far better than going down to the ground floor with a security team if one of them needed a wee in the middle of the night.

"So did you enjoy my version of wild sex last night?" Ivan asked. He looked a little nervous.

"Of course I did," I replied, "I can truthfully say it was the best sex I've ever had." He looked extremely pleased with himself. "I'm as stiff as a board now though." He patted my hand affectionately.

"Would you consider something for me?" I nodded in reply. "Would you get checked for sexual health, as will I, and we ditch the condoms? I take it you're on birth control?"

"I had a shot on Saturday. It takes a week to take effect. I think as long as both of us are checked, then yes, I could do that."

"I'll arrange it for after work today." Ivan looked happy.

Back at the flat, I soothed my aching muscles with a long, hot shower, and got myself ready. Directly after the negotiation meeting, I had arranged lunch with Joan Lester, over in the West End, then it would be back to the office to hopefully draft a contract for the publishing acquisition. I slicked on some lipstick and waited for Roger to buzz for me.

Justine Moran was a woman I could definitely admire. She had built her publishing company from scratch to become a major player in cookery and lifestyle books. With four of the top ten bestselling titles in her stable, she was cash rich, and looking to expand. We were meeting the owner of a small publishing house which specialised in niche books for the catering industry, and cookery schools. Justin's explained that by combining the two catalogues, there would be scope for cross-selling, and also author collaboration.

At nine thirty prompt, a short, fat man arrived, and was introduced as Daniel Fielding. He was the owner of Field and Mortimer publishing, the company Justine hoped to buy. We sat down in her office, where I was introduced. I seemed to make him nervous, as he asked Justine why she needed her lawyer present.

"I'll be drawing up the contract of sale, so it's far easier if I sit in on your meeting," I explained.

"Surely we just tell you how much, and what's included, and it's straightforward?" Daniel said, frowning.

"Yes, of course, but sometimes details can be overlooked, and my job is to ensure that they're not." I smiled as I spoke, trying to reassure him. He didn't look comfortable. Justine opened the negotiations, and between them, they worked out exactly what was included in the sale. As Justine didn't need his premises, it mainly came down to his catalogue and copyrights, which Daniel seemed to want a vast amount of money for. I cringed slightly when he maintained that he still wanted income from the copyrights, even though he was selling them. Basically, he wanted a large sum of money for giving up nothing, and I could see Justine getting frustrated too. I prompted a break, ostensibly so Justine and I could check some figures, and while Daniel went outside for a cigarette, I gave her a hard stare.

"The man's a pillock. Wants you to give him half a mill, and keep hold of the royalties. There's no way you can agree to that. His profit for the last three years has never even gone above a hundred grand. This is not a good deal in any way, and I'd urge you strongly to pull out. The company is not worth half a mill, let alone providing a residual income."

"I know, but there are two authors in his stable who I want in mine. This seemed to be the best way to get them."

"Have you tried luring them? A lot cheaper than paying off this idiot for evermore." I countered.

"I tried once, both said no. Said they were happy where they were."

"So try again, dangle a hefty golden hello in front of their noses, everyone has a price. Start with fifty grand each, and go up. Still a hell of a lot cheaper than this deal. Easier going forward too. Are they on a contract do you know? A five book deal or anything?"

She shook her head. "No, there was nothing to stop them apart from a misplaced sense of loyalty."

"Ok. As your lawyer, I'd advise you against this deal. I could also approach these two authors for you, and negotiate a deal with each."

"Ok Elle, let's do this your way."

Daniel did not look happy when Justine pulled out of the deal. She explained that she couldn't offer more than two years profit, and no further royalties. Daniel huffed and puffed, telling her what a valuable opportunity she was missing, but still maintaining that he would want income for evermore. By eleven, it was clear there was no deal happening, and he left disappointed. I took the contact details of the two authors, and left for the West End, calling each of them on the way to set up dinner, and sound them out.

Lunch with Joan was a blast. She wanted to acquire an ailing magazine, and revamp it. The current owners were desperate to sell, and were happy to let it go for a song, and guaranteed jobs for their staff. My job would be to prepare a contract of sale, dot the i's and cross the t's. All pretty straightforward. In the meantime, she wanted to know about Ivan.

I found out that they had met several times before, at various functions, and she thought he was the most charismatic man on the planet. She pumped me for information like a goofy fangirl.

"What's he like as a person? I mean, is he fun to be with?"

"He's a lot of fun, and surprisingly nice. A gentleman really." I thought about him tickling Bella that morning, her fat tummy presented to him, and a look of pure happiness on her face.

"So how do you cope with every woman he meets swooning over him? I mean, there's not many men that good looking and rich. Do you worry that he'll stray?"

I frowned, "No. Why would I spend my time worrying about that? If he wants someone else, then it would mean that he wasn't into me, and we should go our separate ways. All the time we're happy together, I'm not going to concern myself."

"He's been called a control freak. Do you find him controlling?" The moment she asked me that question, I twigged.

"Joan, why are you interviewing me?" She had the grace to blush.

"We are printing a story by Dascha Meranov next month. She's claiming he made her life hell, and it took Dascha several years to escape his clutches. I wanted your take on it."

"I'm not at liberty to discuss Ivan's private affairs, and I don't know the story of him and Dascha. You need to go through his press agent. Now, do you really want me to handle this contract, or was it just a ploy to get me here?"

"I thought it was the best way to get you talking, but if we do acquire any other titles, I'll definitely call on you." *Fucking time waster.*

"Ok Joan. I'm going to leave, as I have a very busy schedule, and I don't take kindly to my time being wasted like this. You'll receive my bill for one hour of consultation in the post. Good day." I grabbed my bag, and walked out. As soon as I was in the car, I called Ivan, and told him what had happened. To my surprise, he seemed to find it funny.

"Very inventive of her. Glad you twigged so quickly, just a shame you didn't get the chance to tell her what a sex god I am. I wouldn't mind that being printed."

"I thought it was appalling, and god only knows what Dascha will say about you. Can't we slap an injunction on this?"

"Elle, the only opinion I care about is yours, and as long as you don't think I'm a cruel or heartless man, then whatever anyone else says doesn't matter."

"Your reputation does matter. People do business with you. Plus I don't really want anyone to assume I'm happily dating a sadist."

He sighed, " alright, if it makes you happy I'll alert my PR, but I know full well they're going to want us to do a cheesy 'at home' type spread in Hello, which I'd rather avoid. Plus it would have implications for your security, so you might want to give that some thought."

"I hadn't thought of that. Just talk to your PR, and see what they say. I'd rather throw down an injunction personally."

"Ok. Talk to you later." He rang off. I sank back in my seat, trying to relax, and throw off my irritation. Within 30 seconds, my phone rang again. It was the police, telling me they had the preliminary findings of the post mortem on mum. It had been an aneurysm in her brain, probably killing her almost instantly. The copper sounded sympathetic, assuring me that they had no suspicions of foul play. He estimated that it would take at least another week or so until her body would be released for a funeral, but as soon as I received the coroner's report, which had been posted, I could register her death. I thanked him for his help, and ended the call.

It felt strange calling mum's phone, but Ray picked up straightaway. No doubt mum had the better phone, or there was still some credit on it, so he was now using it. I told him about the call from the police, and enquired how many people would be coming to the funeral.

"At least 50 I should think. She was popular on the estate, people are devastated about what happened. I asked the landlord of the Guy Earl of Warwick if we could have the wake there. He said it'd be fine, he'll even lay on sandwiches, if you want them that is."

"That sounds fine. I'll organise all the paperwork, and undertaker, and let you know when it is. Did you sort out the tenancy of the flat?"

"I did. I'm really grateful to you for that Elle, tenancies are like gold dust, and this is a great flat, one of the best," I cringed, "are you sure you don't want any of the furniture?"

"You keep it Ray, I haven't got room for it. Can you organise invites then? Once I set the date, and we keep it to fifty people only yeah? I don't want a huge bar bill."

"Make it a paid bar, otherwise they'll drink it dry," double cringe, "you know what the greedy bastards are like." *I know what a greedy pig you'd be.*

"Ok. I'll call you when I know more."

Back at the office, I briefed Lewis on my rather disastrous morning, and booked Friday afternoon off to travel to Woolwich to register mum's death, and visit the undertaker. I called the Co-op funeral service in Welling, and booked an appointment.

After making myself a coffee, I settled myself in my office, and began working my way through the dozens of emails that had arrived that morning, answering them methodically. I was pleased to see that the float had been publicised, and initial expressions of interest were being collected from institutional investors. I forwarded the email to Steve Robbins, to keep him in the loop, adding some notes of my own. With no work from Ivan, Paul's project in hand, and Mr Carey handling the work for Goldings, I found myself at a bit of a loose end. I decided to research the two authors that Justine was trying to poach.

Both appeared to have had very minor success with books on baking, and bread making. Neither seemed to be well marketed, or have a great web presence. I looked the first up on Amazon, and his ranking was 450000th in the list. Idly, I wondered how many books per week that equated to. I doubted if it was enough to justify a vast advance. Puzzled, I called Justine to ask why she felt these authors were so valuable. She explained that they had both written textbooks used in cookery schools, which were sold direct, and so had no bearing on their Amazon rankings. It still didn't ring quite right, but I accepted her explanation and informed her that I was meeting them both separately the following week. She authorised me to offer up to £75k each as a golden hello, should they agree to jump ship to Justine's company. Thankfully, neither writer had a literary agent to complicate matters, so I was fairly confident.

I wrapped up at five, and began to make my way back home, only to see the Mercedes waiting outside my flat. Roger hopped out, and informed me that Ivan had booked me an appointment at Harley Street at six. I gave me just enough time for a super quick shower and change. Within ten minutes, I was on my way.

"Why didn't you call and let me know about this?" I asked Ivan when he finally answered his phone.

"Mad busy day," he barked, "I'll be there as quick as I can," before ringing off. *So. Bloody. Rude.*

I was booked in to see a rather stern and disapproving looking lady doctor. She was one of those tall, willowy, rather sullen looking women, with thick glasses, and a superior air. She quizzed me on my general health, and medical history, before giving me a brief examination, and taking blood and urine tests. She peered over her glasses as she told me she would call me with the results on Thursday. Thanking her rather insincerely, I headed back to the car, where Roger informed me that I had been instructed to wait for Ivan.

"I think it would have been nice for Ivan to have asked me to wait himself, Roger. Now are you going to take me home, or should I call a taxi?" Roger looked a bit panicked, and held a finger up as he made a call. I tapped my foot impatiently.

"I'll take you home," said Roger, finally. "Mr Porenski is held up in West London, and sends his apologies. He will call you when he has seen his physician."

Back home, I poured myself a glass of wine, and heated up the slightly congealed lasagne. It tasted a bit past it's best, but I was hungry, so polished it off. I did a bit of housework and laundry, and waited.....and waited. By half nine, there was no sign of Ivan, so I gathered up my book, and got into bed.

I had got right into the story when my phone rang. I was surprised to see from the screen that it was Oscar.

"Switch the news on quick," he said. I jumped out of bed, and turned on the telly. Sky news or beeb?" I asked.

"Sky's probably your best bet." I found the channel, and watched as Ivan left the Conde Nast head office as its new owner, with Dascha on his arm, smiling triumphantly at the cameras. "Are you alright?" Oscar asked.

"Yeah, I'm ok, just a bit...disappointed." I replied, using all my self control to stop my voice from cracking. They looked impossibly gorgeous together, both imperious and charismatic. I felt like a small, brown, country mouse in comparison. I ended the call to Oscar, thanking him for alerting me, and headed back to bed to sob in privacy. Ivan didn't call.

The next morning, I dragged myself to the gym, and ran for the full forty minutes, until my legs were like jelly, and sweat was pouring off me. I followed my beloved routine, taking comfort in the discipline required to be perfectly turned out and professional looking, however, I did wear a suit that I bought myself. I couldn't bear to wear anything Ivan had bought me, even tucking the Prada bag away in my closet, and using my black bag from Next instead. I was in my office, and at my desk by 7.30, with my chin up, and my emotions firmly stuffed into an iron box.

Lewis poked his head round my door, "got a minute?" He said, before plonking himself down in the chair opposite. "I saw the news last night. Have you heard anything from him?"

"No. I'm assuming his in house team handled the acquisition. I wasn't instructed on it."

"That's not what I meant Elle," he said softly, "he introduced you as his girlfriend a week ago. I'm assuming you didn't know he'd gone back to that Russian woman."

"On the news, they said she was his long term girlfriend," I said, "I must have just been the short term one. Anyway Lewis, it's better to find out now, early on, than later when I'm in deeper. I knew he'd never stay with me." Lewis looked surprised. "He's a beautiful billionaire Lewis, he can take his pick. He only wanted me because I kept saying no."

"Personally, I find that hard to believe, I've got no idea why he's done this to you, all I can say is that I'm sorry, and I hope this doesn't put the company in a difficult position with our dealings with him."

"I'll make sure it doesn't. I refuse to allow my personal feelings to effect my work. I still have a superb professional relationship with Oscar Golding, despite a previous relationship."

"I hope so Elle. He opened a lot of doors for you, so do your best to keep him on side, even though I wouldn't blame you for kicking him in the balls." Lewis gave me a small smile, and left.

I spent the day doing paperwork, mainly for Goldings bank. I sat in with Mr Carey, and he explained the protocols for bank audits, and the elements of the banking code that were relevant to a privately owned entity, as opposed to a PLC. I was grateful for the diversion that such detailed work provided. I worked through lunch, and didn't even look at the clock until 7 that evening. I shut down my computer, and headed home, grateful to see Roger waiting outside, but puzzled as to why Ivan would still have his staff ferrying me around.

I heated up a ready meal, and poured a glass of wine, as I contemplated the envelope I'd placed on the island, clearly marked 'Coroner's office'. Fortified by the alcohol, I opened it. I read that the verdict of the post mortem was that mum had died of a brain aneurysm, and that her body had been cleared for funeral arrangements to be made. Seeing it written in black and white slammed it home to me. It really had happened, and I was truly alone in the world. The dam burst, and the tears began to flow, until I was sobbing, sorry for both her, and myself.

I must have cried for a full hour, until I was left with dry, heaving sobs. I glugged a large glass of wine, and picked at the awful ready meal. At nine, my phone rang. It was Ivan.

"Hello Ivan, what can I do for you?" I asked, trying to keep my voice steady.

"I need to see you," he replied.

"Certainly. Would Smollenskis at 8am suit?" I asked.

"I need to see you before that."

"I'm sorry, I'm not available. What's so important that it can't wait till tomorrow?"

"Elle, don't be like this. I need to explain to you. I'm taking it that you saw the news last night?"

"Yes I did. Congratulations on your acquisition. So... Do you need me to meet you at eight or not?"

"No. I need to see you now. There's a lot I need to explain to you."

"No need. I understand what happened. You just do as you wish. It's a bit late for explanations."

"Elle, be reasonable, and give me the chance to explain." I didn't answer. "You don't get to dictate what companies I buy, where I go, or who I have to see, or do business with. Now I've

82

asked nicely. If you insist on being childish, and refusing to see me, then you end up the loser." He was beginning to lose his temper. I flinched slightly as he began to shout down the phone. I didn't reply to him, I just cut the call, turned my phone off, and went to bed. I could go back to being strong, assertive Elle tomorrow, as that night, I needed to hide away from the world.

I lay in bed, and sobbed my heart out.

Chapter 8

There was an email from Ivan on my screen as soon as I got into work the following morning.

From: Ivan Porenski
To: Elle Reynolds
11th June 2013
Subject: Explanation

Elle

My purchase of Conde Nast was designed to stop the publication of the article that you were so concerned about. My appearance with Dascha has put paid to her attempts to smear my character, and it also keeps you out of the limelight, so puts paid to the security issues that come with being my girlfriend, and also any rumours among your colleagues that you are only with me to further your own ambitions professionally. I probably should have told you what was going on, but we were working to get the deal done quickly, so I apologise that you had to find out via the evening news.

I didn't appreciate your rather juvenile refusal to see me last night. I would have rather told you all this in person, rather than having to send you an email.

I have some TUPE work I need doing at Conde Nast, which I would like you to oversee. Please contact Mr Ranenkiov for further instruction on that. You have his number.

I should be available this evening, if you would like to come over to my apartment.

Regards
Ivan

I read and re-read the email several times, trying not to read tone into it. Eventually I drafted a reply. I wanted to scream LIAR at him, but restrained myself. As it was, I was insulted that he clearly thought I was stupid enough to believe a pack of lies.

From: Elle Reynolds
To: Ivan Porenski
11th June 2013
Subject: your email

Thank you for your explanation as to why I found out via the evening news that you have a long term girlfriend. As I have no desire to be a short term girlfriend, bit on the side, or dirty little secret, it does indeed ensure my safety, as I am no longer involved with you in any other way than my professional capacity.
I will contact Mr Ranenkiov this morning regarding the TUPE work.

Thank you for the invitation, which I will have to decline. In my experience, personal and professional don't mix terribly well. I hope we can continue to work well together.

Regards

Elle Reynolds

I pressed send, and got on with some of the work for Goldings. At nine, I picked up the phone and called Mr Ranenkiov, the director of HR for Retinski. He was his usual charming self, and we arranged to meet in my office at eleven to discuss his requirements at Conde Nast. I didn't hear any more from Ivan, so tried to put it to the back of my mind, and concentrate on the task at hand.

Mr Ranenkiov arrived dead on time. He shook my hand warmly, and sat down to run through the list of requirements. I had liked him from the first time I'd met him. He was sharply intelligent, but warm and pleasant, and came over as a great communicator, able to put his requirements across in a concise, exact way.

As Conde Nast had a substantial HR department already, I would simply oversee the transition to Retinski's system. It had been estimated to take around two days, as their computer system was fairly compatible with the one used by Retinski, and their paperwork was in good order.

"Your role will be mainly observational. Making sure any questions are answered, and procedures are followed."

"That's fine, but I'm surprised by this. Surely one of your in house team would be better placed?"

"Ivan wants you to do it. I didn't ask why, although he's like a bear with a sore head today. Any idea what's upset him?"

"No idea," I dismissed, "I haven't seen him. So, when do you want me over there?"

"Can you do Monday and Tuesday next week?"

I checked my calendar, "yep, that shouldn't be a problem." I blocked those days out of my schedule, while he took a file from his briefcase.

"All the details are in here, along with some information you may need, plus the address and directions." I thanked him, and we shook hands. After he left, I studied the file, and concluding that it all seemed rather straightforward, and I wondered why on earth Ivan would pay Pearson Hardwick day rates for such a simple project. I also struggled to get my head around why Ivan would buy a publication, and a whole lifestyle brand, rather than slap an injunction on it. It really didn't make sense.

I had a call that afternoon from the doctor, confirming that all was fine, and a letter was in the post. She also enquired as to where she should send her bill. I paid it there and then using my debit card. There was no way I was letting Ivan pay it, even though it had been his idea. I wouldn't even be using the information, so it felt like a waste of two hundred and fifty quid. *Live and learn,* I thought to myself.

I headed home around seven, pausing at the deli to buy some milk and a sandwich, fully prepared to spend my evening lost in Jeffery Archer's imagination. I was actually rather looking forward to it. After all my recent dramas, I needed some quiet time. I also needed some time without a man. I had found both Oscar and Ivan high maintenance, and rather draining. I was used to my own company, and although I'd had friends at school and uni, I wasn't one to spend lots of time out socialising. I decided to look up a few old pals, and arrange some nights out that didn't involve power crazed men.

I made a latte, changed into my pyjamas, and checked through my post. I noticed one for James with an Australian postmark. I frowned slightly, before adding it to the pile I was leaving on his desk, hoping it wasn't from Janine, as it would only upset him. I had just eaten my sandwich, when there was a knock on the door. I opened it to see Oscar standing there, a worried look on his face.

"Hiya, come in, what can I do for you?" I said, not acknowledging the fact that I was wearing pink jimjams.

"Are you ok?"

I frowned, "of course I am. Why wouldn't I be?"

"All the events this week. It can't have been easy for you."

"I think I'm still in the shock stage over mum. I got the results of the post mortem. It was an aneurysm as they thought. I'm going to register her death tomorrow, and arrange the funeral. I'm coping though."

"And what about Ivan?"

"Over. Still working for him. Doubt if he'll be bothering me much though, as I can pretty much deal with his staff for the type of work we do for him."

"How do you feel about it though?"

I thought about it for a moment. "Relieved if I'm honest. I always knew I was too ordinary for him, and I suspected it was the thrill of the chase for him. I'm not cut out to be a billionaire's girlfriend, so yeah, glad to be out of it."

Oscar scowled at me, and I realised I had ruled him out too. In truth, both men were way too complicated for me, and it was a relief to shed the sense of inadequacy I felt around both of them.

"Ivan isn't seeing Dascha you know. He can't abide the woman."

"He looked pretty comfortable with her hanging off his arm the other night. Besides, I really don't want to discuss this with you, so unless you have a legal problem, I need to make some phone calls, and head to bed."

"Mother suggested I invited you to Conniscliffe this weekend. There won't be anyone else coming. She suggested it might be a nice mini break for you."

"Don't you find it surprising that your mother is so nice to me?"

He shrugged, "not really. You are quite likeable. I think she 'gets' that you're different, and was impressed by the way you handled a difficult test of your integrity. She might be a bit of a gorgon, but she's really quite sharp."

"She's nobody's fool, I'll give her that. I tell you what Oscar, I'd love to visit this weekend, but the caveat is separate bedrooms, and no assumptions that I'm going back to you, I'm not, and you need to accept that."

He nodded, "of course. I'll let mother know about this weekend, she'll be delighted. We'll go after work tomorrow if that's ok?"

"Ok, great, and Oscar?" He looked expectant, "thanks for not judging me over Ivan." He gave me a sympathetic smile, and left.

I decided against phoning old friends, as I'd be away the weekend, so decided on a bath and an early night instead. I had just got into bed when Ivan called. I decided not to answer it, quarter to ten at night was veering towards booty call territory, and I wasn't going to be available. He called twice more before he took the hint that I wasn't picking up.

The next morning I did my usual routine, but had a strange sensation of being watched. I couldn't put my finger on it, a sort of prickling sensation at the back of my neck that caused me to turn around, as if there would be someone there. I experienced it from the moment I left the flat, until I got into my office. I told myself it was probably one of Ivan's team keeping tabs on me, instructed to do so by Mr Control Freak himself. He really had no concept of privacy.

I had a busy morning, full of meetings, and before I knew it, one o'clock had rolled round, and it was time to head off to the Registry of Births, Deaths and Marriages in Woolwich. Laura had organised a taxi for me, which would wait, and take me to my appointment with the funeral directors before bringing me home.

As soon as I left the office, the strange 'being watched' sensation began again. I looked around before getting into the taxi, but nothing seemed amiss. The driver had his ID, and was a regular with the car service that the company used. He chatted about the weather as we headed to Woolwich, but I wasn't paying attention, as I kept checking the side mirror to see if we were being followed.

He waited outside while I registered mum's death, producing the coroners letter as proof of cause. It was a shocking moment, seeing your parent's death certificate for the first time. I got three copies, and stuffed them in my handbag, wanting to get out of there.

As I left the registry, I was certain I caught a glimpse of a man watching me. I couldn't be sure, it was so fleeting, one moment there, then gone in the blink of an eye. I hurried back to the car, and watched behind us all the way to Welling. By the time we got there, I was convinced we were being tailed by a maroon van. I quickly ducked into the undertakers, and arranged the funeral for two weeks time. I had decided on a cremation at Eltham crematorium, and booked the larger chapel in case Ray got carried away with the invites.

It took nearly an hour to sort all the details out and get them booked. I was nervy, and jumpy, half expecting someone to burst through the door any moment. I thanked the undertaker for all his help, and checked the street outside before jumping into the waiting car. We pulled away, heading towards Shooters Hill, and checking behind us, I caught a glimpse of a maroon van about four cars back.

My hands were shaking as I pressed the speed dial for Ivan's number. He picked up on the second ring. "Are you having me followed?" I demanded. Silence. "Are you still there?" I asked.

"Yes, I'm still here."

"Well?"

"There is a security team assigned to your safety, yes."

"In a maroon van, currently in Welling?"

"You're not supposed to spot them," he said sulkily.

"Call them off NOW," I yelled, "and don't you DARE do that to me again. I nearly had a heart attack. Thought I was about to be kidnapped."

"They're only ensuring your safety."

"I'm perfectly safe Ivan. I don't need creepy men following me around thank you. I suggest you call them now, and tell them to leave me alone. If they persist in stalking me, I'll get this cab to pull over at the nearest police station. I'm not your girlfriend Ivan, you can't do stuff like this."

"Here's the thing Elle, if you'd have actually talked to me this week, you would have realised that most of my actions have been to keep you safe. From keeping Dascha happy, to buying controlling share of Conde Nast, and asking you to go there next week. It's all to keep you safe. We had a specific threat to your safety, so will you just indulge me for once, and let me deal with this?"

"Specific threat? Tell me exactly what that means please."

"A message was sent to us...."

"Keep talking."

"Basically saying you were at risk.."

"Of what?"

"Kidnap."

"Is that all?"

He paused, "no. They planned to hold you hostage."

"Who?"

"Russian mafia."

"Why?"

"Because Dascha cannot bear the fact I left her. She is jealous of you beyond all reason."

"So she's bullying you into fucking her?"

He laughed, "I couldn't fuck her if I tried. My dick does get a say in these things you know. She did the article to provoke me. Now I could have used an injunction and wrapped you in security, but she would have just gone to another paper or magazine, and dragged your name into it. By doing as she asked, I made sure no other publication would touch me. By publicly acknowledging Dascha,, and doing this deal for her, I'm keeping you as safe as possible. This problem should be solved by Wednesday, but until then, I need to make sure you're safe and protected."

"Ivan, this is mad. Give me the note, and I'll go to the police."

"That's the quickest way to get killed Elle. They won't mess about."

"So what does Dascha want? To marry you? To fuck you? You can't just play along with this forever."

"Oh, she doesn't want me. She wants Conde Nast. They wouldn't sell to her. I had to buy it using her father's money, get it sorted, which is where you come in, then give it to her as a goodbye gift."

"So if you don't, I get splatted?"

"Yes. So until this deals done, you're not safe. You're her insurance policy that I won't renege on the deal."

"Why the hell are you sending me in there on Monday then?"

"It's the safest place. She won't hurt you there, but she wants you within reach as an insurance policy. By Tuesday night at the latest, the deal will be done."

"Ivan, this is horrendous, you do realise that don't you? Plus you have lied and lied to me over this."

He sighed, "yes I do, but it's not unusual in Russia. Business is much more....brutal. I'm sorry I didn't tell you the truth from the start."

"So why am I changing everything over to Retinski, if it changes again Wednesday?"

"You're not. You're changing everything over to a shell company I currently hold. Ownership of that will change to Dascha. That way, there won't need to be further changes. The press will be told that Dascha and I have split, and the media company is my parting gift to her. So I get my freedom, and she gets her company."

"And I get to keep my face in the same order it is now? Oh great Ivan. I cannot believe I've been dragged into this. I'm appalled. I'm supposed to be away this weekend, I suppose you're going to want to lock me inside my flat now."

"Where are you going?"

"Lady Golding has invited me to Conniscliffe for a mini break."

"Actually that's a great idea. At least you'll be safe there."

"How do you know?"

"They keep billions worth of art safe there, so I'm pretty sure it's secure. I will give Oscar a call and let him know. He may want to increase the security."

"Ivan, I'm disgusted with you. This is not how I live my life you know."

"I know. I'm sorry. Are you going straight home, or back to work?"

"Home."

"Security will be waiting, headed by Roger. They will check your flat, and guard you until Oscar gets there."

"Ok." Ivan cut the call. I sat reeling in the taxi, a million questions racing through my head.

Back home, Roger and another man, who was introduced as Nico, accompanied me up to my apartment, to do a sweep before I was allowed in. When they were happy everything was ok, they waved me in, told me to lock the door, and that they would be just outside.

I had a quick shower, and dressed in jeans and a T-shirt, before packing my weekend bag with two cocktail dresses, and a selection of casual wear. I made a latte, and sorted out my handbag, taking out the paperwork relating to mum, and her funeral. I checked that I had my phone charged up, and some cash in my purse, before slipping my novel in my handbag in case I had some spare time. At five, there was a knock on the door. "Who is it?" I called out.

"Oscar." I opened the door to see a scowling Oscar, flanked by Roger and Nico. "You ready?"

"Yep. Can you take my bag please, and I'll lock up." I carefully double locked the door, and Roger promised he would check on the flat over the weekend for me.

"Follow me for the first five miles please. Make sure we're not followed by anyone else." Oscar said.

"Certainly sir." Roger replied, as he opened the door of Oscar's Range Rover. "Lock the doors when you are both inside please."

They followed us until we were on the A21, and heading through Kent. Both Oscar and I breathed a sigh of relief when the Mercedes peeled off the road behind us.

"Ivan called me, although I already knew what happened. We have some extra security at the castle, although given that it's a castle, it's pretty safe."

"I'm horrified by the whole thing. I wish I'd never set eyes on Ivan. I'm sorry you've been lumbered."

"I haven't been lumbered Elle. I'm delighted to have your company for a weekend. I'm sorry that you got dragged into Ivan and Dascha's drama. I think he's genuinely upset and worried that you're in danger. Dascha is a really toxic and unpleasant girl. She only asked me to that ball to try and convince me to front that bid for her."

"So how come you didn't do it?"

"She had no leverage over me. I didn't want to sleep with her, she had no idea about you and I, and there was no way of her getting a hold over me. No Achilles heel.... that she knew about anyway," he added.

"So she went for Ivan."

"Yep. Knew he'd do if it she threatened you. She has some unpleasant connections I gather."

"I'm surprised they didn't go after his dogs, they're the girls he loves most in the world."

"You haven't seen the size of their security team. They have more bodyguards than Ivan. Dascha, or her thugs, wouldn't be able to get to them."

"All this to buy a magazine. It seems....mental."

"I agree. Dascha wants to be a fashion leader, to be a Queen Bee in the fashion world. At the moment, nobody gives a hoot about her. She thinks as owner of Vogue, people will give her the respect she craves. She's a spoiled little rich girl, who's daddy will indulge her every whim. This is costing him nearly five billion quid. He must be mad. Conde Nast is a large luxury brand, not just Vogue magazine, and she won't have a clue how to run it all. I don't think she's thought about that."

"Why wouldn't they sell to her, or her father? I don't get why it had to be fronted."

"I gather there's been some bad blood in the past. The family consortium that owned it refused to even speak to Dascha or her father, he has quite a reputation as a thug. They sold to Ivan based on the fact he was no longer with her. When she showed up after the sale and told the reporters she was his girlfriend, well, they weren't happy."

"I bet. That's his reputation shot then."

"Not really. He didn't say who he was or wasn't seeing. They just assumed. That's what he told me." I thought about my almost-lunch with Joan Lester.

"Oscar, what if he reneges, and lets them get me? He might have only asked me out to set this deal up."

"Do you believe that?"

I thought about it. "No, but I wouldn't put it past him."

"I would. He wouldn't be breaking his neck to keep you safe if he was planning to let them have you."

We drove on in silence. I watched Oscar drive, handling the large car smoothly and confidently. It struck me how solid and dependable he had proved himself to be, despite the fact that I had left him, and gone out with someone else.

Oscar broke the silence. "How did it go at the undertakers today?"

"Yeah, all organised for two weeks today. It was horrible seeing her death certificate though, very surreal. I'm having her cremated rather than buried. Ray's organised the wake, which sounds as though it'll be horrific. He's having it in the pub, with sandwiches laid on."

"It doesn't matter Elle. It only matters that people pay their respects, and say goodbye. Don't get hung up on it."

I glanced across at Oscar. "How would you know? I bet you've never been to a working class wake."

"You're right, I haven't. I have experienced losing a parent though. In my case I felt so sad for my father having spent his life acquiring, looking after, and collecting 'things'. He never actually had any fun. He couldn't dance, he was so stiff and repressed that he could barely move. His life was stifled by his great wealth, and the need to preserve it. I swore that I would enjoy my life, and enjoy the money, rather than be its slave.

When he died, the funeral was held in the chapel in the grounds, and it was all business people and fellow aristocrats. All frozen in fear. A bit like my mother, so fearful of being common that she never actually experiences much happiness."

"You're a superb dancer. I loved watching you."

"I made sure I could. Practiced a lot as a teenager. Even took classes at one point."

"All I did was dance to Top Of The Pops, and visit the youth club at the end of our road. I never did the tap and ballet classes when I was little. Too busy sticking my little nose into books for all that. Every week, mum would take me to the library to choose our books for the week. She'd get some historical romances, and I'd read Just William or Mallory Towers, and dream of going to boarding school."

"Well I went to one, and I can assure you it was nothing like Just William. It was always freezing, horrifically brutal, and the food was swill. Not so much midnight feasts, more late night crying and masturbation contests. I credit Eton for fucking me up emotionally. Lots of the old boys never manage to achieve happy marriages, most of them are too screwed up."

"Why do public schoolboys have a reputation of being emotionally stunted with women?" I was curious.

Oscar thought for a moment, "I think it was drummed into us that we were superior, both in terms of lesser men, and all women. Plus of course, girls were forbidden fruit. Touch a girl, you got expelled, but bugger each other, and you got a slapped wrist. I suppose if you're told in your formative years that sex with a woman is the worst thing you can do, it kind of stays with you."

Chapter 9

When the gates closed behind us at Conniscliffe, I breathed a sigh of relief. The castle looked solid and safe, rather like Oscar at that moment. Jones took my bag, and we followed him in.

"I put you in the room next door to mine, just in case," said Oscar, steering me into the drawing room. "Mothers gone to a women's institute meeting, but said to tell you she'd see you in the morning."

"Ok, so what's the plan for tonight?" I asked. Oscar looked quizzical.

"Whatever you like. I can show you more of the castle, we can play billiards, watch a film, you tell me what you'd like."

"I'd love to see more of the castle, if that's ok."

"Sure. I arranged to eat quite early, so I'll take you on the guided tour afterwards. Now, glass of wine?"

"Please." Oscar went and found Jones to ask for our drinks.

"Do you want me to get changed for dinner?"

"Not tonight, it's only the two of us, so no need to stand on ceremony."

"Do you eat in the big dining room when you're here alone?"

Oscar laughed, "no, I eat in the snug with a tray on my lap, watching television. Did you think I put a suit on and sit in silence at the table all on my own?" I shrugged. "Is that where you'd like to eat this evening?"

"That would be lovely. I feel like I've not relaxed all week. A soft sofa, and some trashy telly sounds wonderful"

"Your wish is my command madam," said Oscar with a smirk.
"Besides, I like Friday night TV." He took my hand, and led me
down a corridor, and into a small sitting room, with three large,
slightly scruffy sofas, a big, low, coffee table in the centre of them,
and a flat screen TV perched on a cabinet, which looked decidedly
non antique. It was the cosiest, most informal room I'd seen at the
castle. I curled up on the sofa, and sipped my wine, as Oscar
flicked through the channels, before settling on the one show.

Before long, Jones arrived with some food on a trolley, along
with two lap trays, and a bottle of wine. It was quite comical
seeing a butler serve dinner on trays as if he was serving at a
dinner party, but I kept quiet. If it was Oscar's idea of relaxed, I
didn't want to mock.

Our roast chicken was delicious, and I was starving. "You
pack it away don't you?" Oscar remarked, "I don't know where you
put it. I like a woman who eats."

"I was starving. I've not eaten at all well this week. With
James away, I've lived on ready meals and sandwiches, plus I've
been a bit stressed."

"Can't you cook?"

"Oh yes. I'm quite a good cook, but I've not had much in the
house, no time to shop, and I hate cooking for just myself. James is
really good at keeping the fridge filled up, and he loves to whip up
nice meals. It's a sort of hobby of his. What about you? Are you
domesticated?" I'd never asked Oscar how he managed during the
week in his apartment before.

"I'm not bad, can manage simple stuff. My cleaning lady
usually shops for me, so considering I grew up with servants, I'm
quite housetrained really."

We were interrupted by Jones, who cleared away our plates,
and served profiteroles for desert, with a small glass of desert wine
to accompany, then returned twenty minutes later with coffees. I
decided having a butler was extremely cool. After dinner, Oscar
showed me around the wine cellars. I had kind of expected one
room, with some wine racks and bottles, but the cellars were vast,
and lined with thousands of bottles.

"Why are there so many bottles down here? You couldn't
drink them all in a lifetime," I said, marvelling at the sheer scale of
it.

"Investment mainly. A lot of these wines appreciate in value, so it's just another way of holding assets. My father built a lot of this collection. I add to it every year by buying fine wines, and laying them down. It means I get to drink good vintages, plus add to the family fortune, so it's a win win." He took my hand, and led me back up a small, stone staircase to the back of the cellars. "These used to be the dungeons. I used to love it down here when I was little, although my sister refused to venture down here again after I dressed up in a bed sheet and jumped out at her. It's quite a spooky place at the best of times."

I shivered slightly. Even in the heat of mid June, it was dank and chilly. "I wouldn't fancy being locked up down here, it's eerie now, let alone in the days before electric lights."

"I would have thought the entire castle was spooky back then. It's a bit scary even now. We have several resident ghosts, and lots of the servants have reported strange happenings over the years."

"Have you ever seen anything?" I asked. Oscar nodded.

"I used to see a young girl, dressed in a sort of maid's dress when I was a child, but not recently. My sister used to see her too. Some of the staff have seen a Tudor man, but I've never seen him. I hear odd noises all the time, but I suppose I'm used to them, so they don't bother me. It's such an old place that it's bound to knock and creak a bit."

"Thanks for that Oscar. I'm gonna be sat up all night with the lights on now." I said, shoving him gently.

"You're not scared of bumps in the night are you Elle?" Oscar smirked. *Bastard.*

"Course not. I'm far too rational for that."

"Good. In which case, I can show you the west wing."

I followed Oscar through myriad corridors, lined in ancient wood panelling. "This wing is pretty much disused, so it's really creepy." He opened a door, and stepped aside to allow me to enter. The furniture was covered in dust sheets, and in the twilight, it looked like the setting for a horror film. He lifted a sheet to reveal a cabinet full of stuffed animals, their faces frozen forever, and their bodies posed stalking, sitting, or mid flight. I shuddered, feeling a chill despite the heat outside.

We explored more of the rooms that made up the west wing of the castle, Oscar explaining what the rooms would have been used for in the days when a vast extended family would have lived there, with dozens of servants. "So is it freezing in the winter?"

"My apartments are centrally heated, as is the apartment my mother uses. My sister's quite hardy, and still uses traditional log fires. I prefer to be warm and comfortable, so have both. The walls are about six foot thick, so it's surprisingly well insulated. We can't have double glazing though, as it's grade one listed, which is a bit of a nuisance."

"Can we go back to the snug? It's unnerving here, and I'm jumpy enough with Dascha's henchmen after me, let alone spectres and ghosts adding to the mix."

Oscar laughed, "oh Elle, I'm sorry. Let's go get you a stiff drink." We wandered back to Oscar's apartments, and back to the snug, where he poured us each a large brandy. We sat quietly, watching a comedy show, and I had begun to relax, when lightning flashed. "Rains started," said Oscar, "typical isn't it? A few days of hot weather, and we get a thunderstorm. At least it'll clear the air though, it's been quite muggy this evening."

Oh this just gets better. In a creepy, haunted castle in a thunderstorm, with maniacs after me. Great.

"I'm never gonna sleep now. Could I have another brandy please?" I wanted to go back to London, where a storm would be a welcome respite to stifling humidity rather than the backdrop to a cheesy horror film. Oscar looked amused as he poured out another large helping of cognac.

"Are you scared of thunderstorms?"

"No. If I was in London, I'd barely notice it. However, I'm hiding from the Russian mafia in an enormous, haunted, and frankly rather creepy old castle, so forgive me for being a touch nervier than normal." I smiled rather wanly.

"Elle, you're totally safe here. Firstly, only Ivan knows you're here, and second, nobody has ever been attacked or killed by a ghost. There's no need to worry. This whole castle is heavily protected, and let's face it, they'd never find which room you were in. There are 200 to choose from. It would take them all night to look."

I relaxed slightly, "I know you're right. I'm just being silly."

"Look it's nearly eleven. Why don't you try and get some sleep?" Oscar yawned, and I noticed that he looked tense, and a bit red eyed. I nodded, and we headed upstairs. He showed me into the bedroom next to his. It was vast, with an emperor sized canopied bed, covered in heavy, red velvet drapes, and a matching bedspread. Oscar closed the curtains, and turned back the covers, before planting a kiss on my forehead, and bidding me goodnight, adding that he would be next door if I needed him. I brushed my teeth, and changed into pyjamas before clambering into the enormous bed, and turning the light off.

I lay in the dark listening to the storm, timing the lightning flashes, and accompanying thunderclaps, and wished I was at home. Every creak made me tense, and I burrowed under the covers to try and block out the sounds. When I heard a thud, I shot out of bed, and ran into Oscar's room. He was sitting up in bed reading, and looked surprised to see me.

"I heard a thud," I said, feeling rather stupid, "and I can't sleep. Can I stay here?" He pulled back the covers, and I got in, and lay on my side facing him. "I'm sorry, I'm being such a girl," I said, scanning his face to try and gauge what he was thinking. He put down his book, and lay facing me. Grasping my hand, he smiled reassuringly.

"You're more than welcome to stay here, better than laying awake all night. The thud was me dropping my book, so nothing to worry about. Try and sleep, and it'll all seem better in the morning." He turned off the light, and lay quietly, still holding my hand.

I woke up completely wrapped around Oscar, practically clinging on to him. He stirred as I peeled myself off his body, and sleepy blue eyes gazed into mine. "Did you manage to sleep in the end?"

"I did, thanks. I'm sorry I disturbed you last night."

"Don't be silly. It was lovely just to hold you again. You had a difficult week, so it was understandable that you needed a cuddle." We lay there a while, not touching, just each lost in our own thoughts. I felt incredibly torn. Oscar felt comfortable and familiar, as well as solid and dependable. He was still handsome and sexy, yet the knowledge that he'd had sex with a man weighed heavily on my mind, plus his other sexual 'quirks' added to the mix, dampened any desire I had for him.

"What are you thinking?" I asked, as he gazed at me.

"That you look lovely all mussed up, and in your pink pyjamas. This might be the last time I get to share a bed with you, so I'm committing it to memory." My heart broke a little as he said it. Oscar wasn't an emotional man, and rather prone to being suspicious or dismissive of women, so this new, softer side was lovely to see. "What are you thinking Elle?"

"That I wish I'd never seen what I did, and that you didn't have the issues that you do."

"I wish that too. I've never wished for anything more than to rewind time to the night before, so that I could have done everything differently. I would have said no to Darius, held you tight, and never let you go."

"There were other issues too. I struggled with some of your quirks. I hated the fact that you seemed to find me distasteful, you know, down there." I blushed as I said it, but his refusal to do cunnilingus had made me feel as though I had been unclean.

"Distasteful? Is that what you thought? Oh Elle, I've never found any part of you less than beautiful. The truth is that I've never tried it, never actually licked a pussy, and like anything, it becomes a habit. Like I said before, public school fucks you up."

"I see. Oh well, I won't take it personally then. So, changing the subject, what shall we do today?"

"There's something I'd love to do, but I'm not sure you'd let me..." Oscar looked apprehensive.

"Go on." *Please don't ask me for a shag.*

"I would love to take you on that shopping trip I promised you."

"I couldn't Oscar, I'd feel like I owed you, and it's not how I want to feel. Ivan bought me that dress and stuff, and I nearly had a bloody meltdown over it. I earn a really good living, and there's nothing I need." He looked disappointed. "How would you feel about me buying you stuff?" He flopped onto his back and thought about it.

"I don't know. It's never happened, so I've got no idea. I'm not trying to buy your affection Elle, I just want to give you a little treat, and make you happy. I like seeing you all polished and sophisticated almost as much as I like seeing you in your pyjamas with your birds nest hair. I hate that Ivan got to do that for you, and I didn't."

"Let's get some tea, and talk about this." I was desperate for a drink, and felt a bit 'put on the spot'. As much as I enjoyed being treated to nice things, I didn't want that awful feeling of being bought and paid for, and I had so many mixed feelings about Oscar that I needed some time to think. Oscar threw on a dressing gown, and passed one of his to me. We went down to the breakfast room to find Mrs Dunton fussing over the tureens, having just made sausage, bacon and eggs. She bustled off to make me a pot of tea, while Oscar helped himself to coffee. We had just sat down to eat when Lady Golding arrived with a cheery smile.

"How lovely to see you again. Oscar told me about the pickle you're in over that dreadful Russian woman. Terrible way for her to behave, especially given your circumstances this week."

"Yes, I'm appalled at it all too. I'm supposed to go to Conde Nast on Monday and oversee some work. I'm dreading it. I'm worried they could snatch me at any time." Lady Golding looked horrified.

"Can't someone else do it, and you stay here until this is all blown over?"

"Apparently Dascha is insisting that Elle is within reach until the deals done. I suggested that too mother. I also offered to put security all around the building until this is over, but Ivan tells me he's already arranged it." Oscar said, looking a little uncomfortable.

"I suggest you put some there anyway, just in case. I don't trust foreigners Oscar. Just the fact that Elle's been dragged into this is bad enough, let alone trusting Podunky to give back a five billion pound company. He's a greedy man, and all it would cost him would be Elle. No, you organise our security to make sure she's not betrayed."

"Of course mother."

"So, have you planned anything for today? It looks like rain, and the forecast isn't very good."

"I wanted to take Elle shopping, but she's not keen. Beyond that, maybe wellies on, and a long walk."

"I thought you liked fashion?" Lady Golding said, frowning slightly.

"I do, but I can buy things for myself, and there's nothing I really need."

"Need never comes into it," she smiled, "he's got nothing to spend his money on, so why not indulge him? Plus it'll be fun in the helicopter. You can trudge through the mud tomorrow."

"Helicopter?" I asked, looking at Oscar.

"Yes, quickest way to get to town and back. I booked it for today." He looked a little sheepish. "Plus it's safer than transporting you by car. I also booked two bodyguards to meet us at Battersea heliport."

"In that case, it would be churlish of me to refuse." I looked up to see Oscar beaming.

"Good. It arrives here at half nine, so could you be showered and ready by then?"

After breakfast, I headed up to my room to get ready. I was just about to get into the shower when Ivan called. "Still in one piece?"

"Of course. Is there something you need?" I was back to professional Elle.

"Elle, please stop being so cold. This isn't my fault you know."

"Really? Well it never happened to me before I met you. Now, if there's no legal issues, I'm just about to jump in the shower. Let me know if there are any developments please."

"In three days, this will all be over."

"Provided you sign that company over of course," I replied. I wasn't convinced that he would.

"Do you think I'd renege on this deal and throw you to the wolves?" He sounded incredulous. I didn't answer. "Elle, how could you possibly think I'd do that to you?"

"It's five billion quid Ivan, and I'm just a girl you've known a few weeks. By your own admission, you want to own the world."

"I don't want to own a world without you in it. What's made you think I'd do the dirty on you?"

"You did. I saw you shark a client once. It doesn't matter what you say or do, I saw it, and I know you did it deliberately, so forgive me for not believing that you're always the good guy. You lied to me over this, so I now have to assume that everything you say is a lie."

"Lying to you at the start of this was a mistake, and I wish I hadn't, but I will keep you safe Elle. I look after what's mine." He sounded panicked.

"I'm not yours Ivan. I don't belong to anyone." I cut the call, reasoning that he never said goodbye anyway. He called back straight away.

"Don't you dare put the phone down on me. I will NOT let Dascha drive you away from me. Let me just deal with this, then I'll figure out a nice treat for you to say sorry for letting this happen to you."

"Keep your money Ivan, and shower it on your next girlfriend. I don't want any gifts, treats or surprises thank you. What I want is a quiet life, with my peace of mind intact, and a boyfriend who doesn't dump me on the news at ten." I clicked off the phone, and put it on silent before heading into the shower.

Oscar and I ended up having a really lovely day. The helicopter landed on the back lawn, and took us to Battersea in less than an hour, with stunning views all the way. A car, driver and bodyguard met us there, and whisked us off to Harrods, where Oscar tried to persuade me to practically buy up the whole store.

We had a gorgeous lunch at the Mandarin Oriental, before heading over to Harvey Nichols for more retail therapy. It was fun in the menswear department, where I insisted on styling a new outfit for Oscar, making him try on uber stylish Prada jeans, and skinny fitted shirts, which he agreed, looked great. I even bought one for him, which made him pout a bit. He loved a Roland Mouret dress I tried on, and insisted on buying it for me in four different colours. We even had afternoon tea in Fortnums, before heading back to Conniscliffe.

Lady Golding greeted us when we hopped out of the helicopter, her helmet of hair not even moving in the strong downdraft. Back in the sitting room, we showed her all our purchases, eliciting oos and ahs from her. I had decided to wear one of my new dresses for work on Monday. If I was going to be kidnapped, at least I'd look good. As I had clothes to wear, I didn't have to return to London Sunday night, and Oscar said he would arrange a driver, and personal protection to pick me up early Monday morning to accompany me to the Conde Nast headquarters.

Oscar excused himself to organise my security arrangements for Monday and Tuesday. While he was in his study, Lady Golding and I had a gin and tonic, and chatted about my day. She looked quite wistful when I told her about our afternoon tea in Fortnums.

"I love that shop," she declared, "they do the best cakes in London, and the tea is always so fresh. I miss those type of things since my husband died. I never seem to go up to London nowadays.

"I could always book an afternoon off, and meet you. I'd love to go back there again."

Her eyes lit up, "I'd really look forward to that. When you are back at work, see when you can arrange, and just let me know. Maybe we could even see a show while I'm there."

"I love theatre. Yes, we'll do that. I'll call you on Wednesday, and we'll arrange it." She looked delighted, and it struck me how lonely it must be for her in a vast castle in the middle of nowhere day in day out, with only Oscar for company at the weekend.

We had dinner in the smaller breakfast room that evening, as Oscar's mum was joining us. None of us bothered to change though, as it was only us three. She was on good form, and entertained me with funny stories about Oscar as a boy, smiling as he groaned at her tales of putting worms in his sister's dolls house, and persuading her to slide down the banisters, which resulted in a trip to hospital to have her broken arm fixed.

After we'd all eaten, she bade us both goodnight, and went back to her own apartment. Oscar and I settled into the snug to watch a film. I began to worry about where I would sleep that night. I really didn't want to sleep alone in the scary bedroom, but I also felt it was a bit unfair to sleep in with Oscar with a no sex rule. I really didn't want to lead him on, as he had proved himself to be a perfect gentleman, and a good friend.

In the end, I needn't have worried, by half ten I was sparko, waking up next morning in my T-shirt and knickers in Oscar's bed, with a sleeping Oscar beside me. I looked at his clock, seeing it was half seven, and swung my legs out from under the covers. "It's Sunday," Oscar muttered, "have a lay in."
I'll go and get us both some drinks, and bring them back up," I said, before wrapping his dressing gown around me and heading down to the kitchen. Mrs Dunton fixed me a tray of tea and coffee pots, and I took them upstairs. Setting the tray down, I poured, and took our drinks over to Oscar's bedside table. He struggled up onto

his elbows and took a sip, while I perched on the edge of the bed. "So, what's the plan for today?"

"I thought a nice walk in the grounds, some lunch, a nap, because you've got me up so bloody early, and maybe a film later. How does that sound?"

"Lovely."

"I spoke to Ivan last night, to let him know you would have extra security on Monday. He's not happy. Accused me of stealing you away. I did point out that you have a say in these things, and I was just trying to keep you safe, given that he put you in harm's way."

"You know my problem? It's when I get treated like a helpless airhead. It grates on me. I didn't fight my way up the ladder by being pathetic or weak, and it pisses me off that he seems to think I'm just an object to be stolen."

"Hmm. Well, he's going to put up with you having security around you. It's not fair to use you as a pawn in a business deal, whoever you end up with."

The day seemed to pass far too quickly, and before I knew it, it was Monday morning, and time to face the music.

Chapter 10

I had a horrible sense of foreboding as we pulled up at Vogue House in Hanover Square. It was an impressive building, and I watched chic, beautiful people pouring in to begin their working day, oblivious to the secret drama that would be happening under their noses. I had put on my Roland Mouret dress as if it was a suit of armour that morning, determined that I wouldn't let any nerves or insecurities show. I took a deep breath, and strode in, flanked by my two bodyguards, courtesy of Oscar.

The girl at the front desk confirmed I had been expected, and I waited while she called someone to come and get me. I looked around the immaculate foyer, taking in the posters showing the Vogue front covers, and other publications in the Conde Nast stable. I didn't have to wait long before an immaculate blonde came striding over. "Ms Reynolds? Good morning, I'm Andrea Mills, the HR director here. I understand that you're here to oversee the changeover for Mr Porenski."

"Pleased to meet you," we shook hands, "yes I'm just here to make sure it all goes smoothly, and on time." She led us over to the lifts, and up to the fourth floor. We chatted on the way up, and she didn't foresee any major problems. All the records were properly kept, and pay rates were to remain the same. Ivan's IT people had been in at the weekend, installed everything, and tested it. She explained that the files had all been copied across, and they were now just checking that everything was copied correctly. I listened, wondering what on earth I was going to do for two days. Andrea appeared highly efficient, and on top of everything.

"Mr Porenski's in the chairman's office, and asked that you attended a meeting with him before coming to check on the personnel department." I tensed at the prospect of seeing Ivan for the first time in a week.

Andrea showed me to his office, and explained that she would be down the corridor in room seven, when I was finished with Ivan. I steeled myself before knocking on his door. To my surprise, he opened it himself. "Elle, glad you're here. Security remain outside please." His bodyguards stepped out of the room, and joined mine just by the door. Ivan closed it, and strode over to the desk. "It feels like I haven't seen you for ages, I've missed you. Please let me hold you." I didn't reply, and stood stock still, not sure what to do. I was torn, Ivan still looked like my beautiful lover, but the fear I'd experienced, and disappointment that he'd put me in harm's way, left me frozen to the spot, unwilling to respond to him. "Elle, what's wrong with you? Come let me hold you."

"No, Mr Porenski. I'd prefer not to. Now, Ms Mills appears to have the changeover under control, so what exactly would you like me to spend the next two days doing?"

"Elle, you can sit and read a book, play on the Internet, anything, as long as you are in this building today and tomorrow." He walked towards me, and I instinctively stepped back.

"Don't touch me," I hissed at him. "You want me here, so I'm here. It doesn't mean that I'm happy about it, or that you get to touch me. I meant what I said, it's professional all the way from now on."

"Are you back with Oscar?" Ivan looked anguished, which surprised me.

"I belong to nobody."

"That's not what I asked. You spent the weekend with him, and he's paying for your security. Are you with him?" I didn't answer. Ivan fixed me with his laser beam glare. "Has he fucked you this weekend? Dammit Elle, put me out of my fucking misery here. It's bad enough that you're involved with this, let alone leaving me over it. Just..just tell me the truth, did he fuck you?"

"It's none of your business Ivan. You lost the right to demand answers when you appeared on television with that creature on your arm, and made me a laughing stock, and when you sent an email that was a lie from start to finish, you lost the right to expect the truth from me."

Ivan banged the desk with his fist. "I will NOT let Dascha drive you away from me, and I will not let Golding steal you. You are mine...please Elle." He looked distraught.

"Ivan, I'm not a possession that can be 'stolen', and you'd do well to remember that. I'm a living, breathing person, who has a say in these things. I'm only here so that this deal happens, and I'm watching you as much as I'm watching the bitch. Now, to ease your mind, no I didn't 'fuck' Oscar this weekend. The last man who 'fucked' me was you, and right now it's something I deeply regret. Now, I'm happy to sit here till five with my security, and read a book, but be aware that there's a bit of me that believes that you'd throw me to the wolves and not give a toss, so think about that when you're shouting at me, and demanding answers." I stood my ground, and had kept my voice low and determined. I refused to let him intimidate me.

He seemed to slump slightly, and looked defeated. "I'm sorry Elle. None of this is your fault, I just can't bear the thought that I could lose you over this."

I raised my eyebrow, "Could? Try have." Ivan stared at me in disbelief. "Now, if you'll excuse me, I'm going to have a look at what your personnel department are doing."

"Don't go, not yet," Ivan pleaded, "we need to resolve this."

"I have resolved it. You're free to be with someone else. I do your legal work, and that's all. There's nothing to debate." I stayed firm, noticing how sad he looked.

"Tell me, did you ever have feelings for me at all?"

"I sobbed like a baby when I saw you on the news with Dascha. So yes, I did, but I'm not dumb enough to think I was ever anything more than a challenge to you."

"Oh Elle, don't let her win. This is exactly what she wants, and what I tried to avoid. Please just have a little faith in me, and let me deal with this, and I'll do anything you want to make it up to you. By tomorrow evening the wretched woman and her slimeball father will be out of our lives."

"Tell me about her father. Who is he?"

"A thug. Huge in mining and minerals. Stole his company really when the old Soviet Union fell apart. Made a hell of a lot of enemies over the years, and is well known for his dubious business practices. Wife was murdered years ago, and Dascha is all he has left. She's almost as unpleasant as him really. They are both bullies."

"Did you love her?"

Ivan sighed, "I was dazzled by her for a while. I thought we would be compatible, both being from Moscow originally, and both being ambitious. Her father liked me, and encouraged me. On paper it should have worked. In reality, I grew to dislike her intensely. For such an indulged woman, she is incredibly mean spirited and envious. The incident with Bella gave me the perfect excuse to end the engagement. If I had told her the truth, that I was leaving her because I felt nothing for her, I would have been killed."

"Is she still in love with you?"

"No. She's not capable of loving anybody but herself. She's a classic psychopath, as is her father. She's currently enjoying tormenting me with what she'll do to you should I renege on this deal, knowing how terrified I am for you."

"So am I being watched?"

"Not as far as I know. I have security all over this building. This deal, by its nature, has had to be totally secret. Only you, me and Oscar know about it. Oscar took care of the money transfers in Switzerland, so there is no money trail. So as far as anyone knows, I bought this with my own money, paid cash, and will give it all to Dascha. If it got out what has really happened, she'd be a laughing stock. At the moment, she has no reason to hurt you, and in some respects, it's in her own interests that you remain safe. She knows that if you go missing before our press conference tomorrow, that our deal's off."

"How come they trust you so much, I mean, it's five billion quid?"

Ivan stared at me for a moment. "They know I'm in love with you."

For a split second, the world stopped turning, as I took in Ivan's words. A bit of me wanted to throw myself into his arms, and cling on to him forever, and another part wanted me to hurt and punish him, as he had done to me. In the end, all I did was gape at him in shock. His beautiful face betrayed a mixture of regret, sadness, and yearning. Did he love me? I believed that he did. How I felt about him was more complicated. I did have feelings for him, possibly not 'in love', but not far off, although I'd felt that he'd stamped all over my heart when I saw him with Dascha, playing the happy boyfriend. Knowing that the whole thing had been faked, somehow changed things.

"Ivan, let's get through the next two days, and see what happens."

He let out a breath he'd been holding. "We can do this Elle," He gave he a small, rather wan smile, and went on, "let's just keep up appearances till this is over, just don't forget how I feel about you."

"I'm going to check on your personnel department. I'll be in room 7 if you need me." I left Ivan standing in the middle of the room.

Andrea was extremely organised, and I liked her enormously. Her systems would rival mine in efficiency, and perfection. Her staff were diligently checking the computer files against the paper files, (which were in perfect order), for anomalies or missing information. She had already emailed all the staff their new contracts, and over 80% had come back signed, entered into the system, and filed. She had even run a simulation for the month end, and was happy that there appeared to be no unexplained differences. I sat beside her as she showed me exactly what had been done, and the list of people still to return their new contracts. All in all, I was impressed.

"It seems everything's in good order. Mr Porenski will be delighted with this. Now, do you have any questions for me?"

"Is he going to be making any significant changes?" Andrea looked a little anxious, which was understandable.

"Not as far as I'm aware. I've not been instructed for any redundancies, if that's what you're asking. You'd be the first to know if he was. As far as I'm concerned, we change everything over to Retinski's holding company, and that's it." She visibly relaxed.

"I was hoping that would be the case, but with takeovers, nobody ever knows if their jobs safe do they?"

"Only when they're not performing, but I can definitely recommend you to Ivan. Your department is run extremely well."

"What's he like to work for?"

"I don't work for him as such, I work for Pearson Hardwick, his legal representatives. His staff all seem to get on with him ok, and he runs his companies very well. He's very exact."

"Good. You know we all thought you were his girlfriend, not that Russian woman. I gather she was talking to one of our journalists about her terrible relationship."

"Did you? No, I'm his lawyer, well, one of them." I was deliberately non committal. "Easy mistake to make, as I'm often trailing along to meetings with him."

"Joan Lester said she met the two of you at a ball, and Ivan introduced you as his girlfriend." She wasn't letting go.

"Well, I suppose it's better than admitting that you drag your lawyer around to charity events. Dascha was there that night, she just arrived separately."

"Oh, I didn't realise....sorry for being nosy." Andrea looked a bit embarrassed.

"It's fine, really. You're not the first person to assume we're an item, but I really am his lawyer." *Not quite a lie, not quite the truth.* "Now, is there an empty office I could occupy?"

"Certainly. Room 11 is free. I'll show you." I followed her down the corridor, with my guards trailing along behind. "Why the security?"

"Ivan insists on it. Not sure why," I lied. She showed me into an office, and promised to send an intern along with tea for both myself, and the security men. I sat down at the desk and opened my laptop. With a complete absence of work to do after I had replied to my emails, I browsed ASOS, and Amazon, ordering the books that Paul had recommended. I also clicked on the link James had sent me to the hotel we would be staying in. It looked gorgeous. A boutique style place, right on the beach near Sotogrande, with a pretty pool and gardens, and a renowned restaurant attached. It looked like heaven, and I gazed at it with longing, desperate for some chill time with my easy going friend, and no mental billionaires making me jumpy.

I was shaken out of my daydreams by a knock on the door. My guard stuck his head in, and announced that Dascha was there to see me. I said yes, but asked if he would stay. She swept in with a sneer on her face. I closed my laptop so she wouldn't see what I'd been looking at, and smiled brightly at her. "Hello Dascha, how nice to see you again. Keeping well I trust?"

"All the better for seeing you, my little insurance policy. Is everything progressing as planned?"

"It is... Andrea Mills is extremely efficient, and everything's in order, and on course to be done by tomorrow."

"Excellent. I would have done it myself, but Ivan positively wore me out last night with his passionate lovemaking. He just couldn't get enough.." She watched for my reaction. *Nice try dozy princess.*

"No problem. We have it all under control here." I smiled sweetly at her scowling face.

"Nice dress by the way, did Ivan buy it for you?" *Oh you have no chance pup beater.*

"No, he didn't. Glad you like it, it's from Roland Mouret's latest collection. I think Harvey Nichols are selling out fast though, so you need to get in quick. Mind you, all the designers will be queuing up to clothe you now." *Take aim.*

"Yes they will. Sadly, Elle, you'll have to carry on finding men to schlep round shops with you."

"Luckily, I can afford to clothe myself. Benefit of having a good job Dascha. I love not being beholden to a man." *And fire.*

She scowled at me, before turning and stalking out of the room. I noticed the security man smirking. I smiled back at him before opening my laptop, and perusing bikinis online.

My next interruption, an hour later, was Andrea, who arrived bearing two cups of tea. I waved the guard out, and she sat down. "What's up?" I asked.

She looked pensive. "Mr Porenski's girlfriend, that's what's up. Do you have any control over her?" I shook my head. "She's asked us to contact all the designers and ask if they want to clothe her. Joan tried to explain that it doesn't work like that, but she won't be told. I gather Joan spoke to someone at McQueen, and they declined straightaway. Behaviour like that could cost us advertisers."

"All I can do is alert Ivan, see if he can curb her enthusiasm. I don't hold out too much hope though." *Bloody glad Ivan will be out of it tomorrow, she'll destroy this place.* I thought to myself.

"Well, see what you can do. Joan needs to protect the advertising revenues, and commanding top designers to clothe her for free wont endear her to anyone, especially with her reputation."

"What have you heard?"

"Just that she's a nasty piece of work, and her father's PR have a job keeping her out of the papers. She's abused her household staff, that type of thing. No designer is going to want to be associated with her."

"I don't envy Joan having to be the one to tell her," I said. Andrea finished her tea, and updated me on progress, before leaving.

I had just ordered a kindle for my holiday, when Ivan came in. "How's it going?"

"Fine. Bored though. Dascha came to say hello, and the HR director's been in to tell me alls fine with the changeover, although Dascha's pissing people off already." Ivan looked quizzical. "Apparently she asked the MD to contact the designers who advertise, and offer them the opportunity to dress her for free. They declined, and Joan's scared to tell her."

Ivan laughed. "I'm not surprised. She's not exactly the darling of the media that she thinks she is. What did she say to you?"

"Just that she was only late because you were shagging her all night. Seeing how bandy her legs were, I couldn't be totally sure she was lying."

"No, they've always been bandy. It's quite pronounced in trousers. You do know she was lying to wind you up don't you?" He looked a bit nervous.

"Oh yes. Don't worry, she won't rattle me. She's way too thick to be a worthy adversary."

Ivan laughed, "Elle, you really are wonderful, you know that? Now, do you have an indication as to what time it will be finished tomorrow? I need to book a press conference, and I need you to prepare a contract giving her the holding company in its entirety."

"Not yet, but I wouldn't be surprised if it was finished today. Andrea Mills is incredibly efficient. Ranenkiov would adore her. I can do the contract now for you. It won't take long."

"Now tonight. What plans have you made?"

"None yet. I might call Oscar, see what he's up to. Maybe he could come round and watch telly with me. I've been a bit jumpy on my own." Ivan's lips flattened into a thin, grumpy line.

"Come round to mine."

"I'm sorry. I don't think that's a good idea, plus I have laundry and stuff to do. I don't have household staff like you, you know." Ivan probably thought the fairies did my washing, and cleaned my flat.

"Tomorrow night then?"

"Let's see how this pans out."

I checked the progress of the HR team, and wrote the contract, printing it off, before leaving at five. With just a couple of employment contracts to come back signed, they were almost done. I bade Andrea goodnight, and headed out to the car. Back at the flat, security did a sweep before allowing me inside, and told me they would be stationed just outside the door. I had called Oscar earlier, who had said he was dining out with some politician that evening, but would be home later if I needed him.

I did some laundry and some housework, before heating up a tin of soup that I found in the cupboard. I had stopped for milk and bread on the way home, but my guards had been jumpy, so I didn't have time to get much. I had relaxed a bit, knowing that Dascha needed me to turn up alive the next morning, so that her deal would go through, although Ivan still had good reason to prevent that. I pondered his admission that he was in love with me. I reasoned that it could have been just a ploy to get me to drop my guard, and trust him enough to allow him close enough to kidnap me and stop the deal. I didn't really know him well, and I couldn't place a bet on it. I didn't believe for one moment that he'd kill me.

I was interrupted by my phone ringing, "hi Ivan, what can I do for you?"

"Can I come over? I want to see you." Alarm bells rang in my head.

"No, not tonight. I'll see you in the morning."

"It's not the same," he purred in his phone sex voice, "it's been a whole week since I last made love to you."

"Well, it's going to be a week and a day then. If this goes through ok, maybe tomorrow night." *Oh I can dangle carrots too Ivan.* "I'm too jumpy and nervous tonight. Surely you understand?"

"Can't I change your mind? I could give you an amazing orgasm. That would relax you, help you sleep." *Yeah, that and rohypnol.*

"No. I'll see you in the morning, assuming I'm still in one piece." I clicked off the phone, mentally slapping myself for considering going back to a man that I believed would cheerfully drug and kidnap me.

Chapter 11

I survived the night alone, but slept fitfully, scenarios racing round my head. I skipped the gym, as it was too risky, and couldn't wait to get back there and burn off a bit of tension. I packed my gym bag, hopeful of a session after work. I dressed carefully, wearing an outfit that Oscar had bought me, with wedge heeled shoes, in case I had to do a runner, and placed my laptop and book in my new Chloe handbag, which was also a purchase from Saturdays shopping extravaganza. At eight o'clock, I left the flat, and joined my guards, who had kept watch all night, for the drive over to Hanover Square.

The traffic was appalling, and it seemed like the whole of west London was gridlocked. I asked my driver to find capital radio so we could find out what the holdup was. It turned out to be an accident, which had been attended to by the air ambulance, and had closed a number of roads around the Hammersmith flyover. I mused that it would have been quicker and easier to take the tube.

We made it to Vogue House at about two minutes to nine. My being late would probably have given Ivan a heart attack, so I was glad to finally be there. I signed in, and made my way up to the fourth floor. Andrea greeted me, beaming. She explained that all employment contracts were back, signed, and the whole system was up and running. I went in search of Ivan to give him the good news.

He was in the chairman's office, talking in Russian on the phone. I waited until he had finished, before informing him that the changeover was complete, and everything was ready.

"Good. Press conference is at ten, downstairs in the meeting hall. I'm just hoping Dascha gets her arse in gear, and doesn't arrive an hour late, as she normally does. I told her to be here by nine, so she should be here by ten. I don't want to keep everything waiting. The sooner this is all over, the better, I've got other things to occupy my time." Ivan looked petulant and grumpy, and the little voice in my head told me that maybe, just maybe, it was because I hadn't gone missing last night. I pulled myself together quickly.

"Anything you need me to do?"

"Just stay at the back of the room. Keep out of her way. As soon as I have made the announcement, I will sign the contract giving her Conde Nast. I will then leave, and you and I meet back at my apartment."

"Ok."

At two minutes to ten, we travelled down to the ground floor. The meeting hall was crammed with press, and there was an air of anticipation in the room as to what was about to be revealed. Ivan didn't often call press conferences. I tucked myself in at the side of the room. Close enough to get a good view, but unobtrusive, and out of Dascha's line of sight. Ivan arrived to a flurry of camera flashes, and smiled at everyone, before taking a seat at the table. "We are just waiting for Dascha Meranov to arrive before we begin," said Ivan, to groans from the photographers.

"So we'll be waiting a couple of hours then," heckled someone at the back. Ivan just looked amused. He looked relaxed as he chatted to the press as they waited, giving nothing away until Dascha arrived. By quarter past, the press were getting edgy, as they had better things to do than wait for a spoilt woman to show up. The conference was interrupted by Nico bounding up to Ivan, and handing him a piece of paper. Ivan read it, his hand flying up to his face, and a look of horror written all over it. He conferred with Nico for a few minutes, before turning, white faced, to the press.

"It's with great sadness that I have to announce the deaths of both Dascha and her father, Vladimir Meranov in a car accident this morning in Hammersmith. I have just found out myself this moment, so forgive me for not being able to furnish you with any detail, and please respect my privacy to grieve. He stood, and strode out of the room, leaving the press yelling out questions.

I turned to my protection officers, "I guess I don't need you now, but would you drive me back to the docklands please?"

I got texts through from both Oscar and Ivan on the way back. Oscar's just enquired as to whether or not I'd heard the news, and Ivan's instructed me to meet him at his apartment. I headed straight there, and was met at the ground floor by his security, and whisked up in the lift. Ivan came barrelling down the hallway as soon as I walked through the front door. He pulled me into a fierce hug, "Thank god you're alright," he breathed.

"Why wouldn't I be? Is there something else you need to tell me?" I frowned.

"No, nothing. They're dead. Nobody will want to harm you now. I'm just relieved it's over." I pulled away from him.

"Ivan, is this anything to do with you? I need to know. I won't judge, I just want you to tell me the truth."

"Oh god, no, nothing to do with me. It doesn't even look like it was a hit. Apparently their driver lost control." He looked into my skeptical eyes, "Elle, you have to believe me. I had nothing to do with it. Besides, there were at least five contracts out on Vlad, as far as I know. If it was a Russian hit, they would have shot them getting out of the car, or poisoned them in Vogue house. The mafia are just henchmen, they wouldn't have the wherewithal or skill to stage a car crash."

"So where does this leave you?"

"Nowhere really. Nobody knows about the deal, apart from you, me and Oscar. I didn't even get that contract out of my pocket, so nobody saw it. Did you delete it from your computer after you wrote it?" I nodded.

"Oscar's mum. She knows. She ordered my security."

Ivan smirked. "She's quite a character, calls me Podunky. She's as sharp as a knife, and wouldn't drop Oscar in it. There is possibly another issue though."

"Go on."

"When we got engaged, Dascha and I both made wills, leaving our estates to each other. I changed mine when we split up. I don't know what she did with hers."

"I see. Who drew it up?"

"Pearson Hardwick. At the head office." Ivan led me into his study, and I sat down before pulling my phone out, and calling Lucy.

"Hi Lucy, it's Elle. I have a strange one for you. Can you look up Dascha Meranov for me. Apparently we wrote her will a few years ago. Can you find out when it was last updated please?"

"Hey babe! Sure, won't take a jiffy. I must come over and see you soon. I want to see if that hunky boyfriend of yours has a twin brother. Hang on.....yup....here it is......last updated 18th June 2011."

"Brilliant," I wrote down the date on the desk pad, "now can you search Vladimir Meranov and see if we hold one for him as well please?"

"Sure, won't be a mo......here we are.....yup, we have it.....dated 30th November 2012. Have they died then?" I wrote down the second date.

"Yes. This morning in a car crash."

"Oh dear, well I'll get them out of storage, and invite the relevant people in. Speak to you soon, ciao baby."

"Bye Luce." I turned to Ivan, "you heard all that?" He nodded. "Have you found out any of the circumstances of their deaths yet? Who died first, that kind of thing?"

"All we've been able to find out is that Vlad died at the scene, and Dascha died on the way to hospital."

"Are you upset?" Ivan gave me a 'don't be stupid' look.

"No. I'm relieved. Both for you, and the girls. Dascha was the only serious threat I really had. I tend to avoid doing business with Russian gangsters these days." He pulled me into a hug, holding me tight and burying his nose in my hair. "I was so scared Elle. Not much frightens me, but the thought of anything happening to you.....she tortured me, said she'd mutilate you...film you being raped, that kind of thing. I've not slept for a week. I worried you'd run back to Oscar, knowing he'd be able to keep you secure. He was worried about your safety too."

"He was a good friend to me this weekend, apart from scaring me senseless on Friday night by telling me ghost stories during a thunderstorm."

"Hmm, probably thought you'd be too scared to sleep alone, and would have to beg to get in with him. He's a sly devil. I never put anything past him. I'm glad he looked after you so well though. He's a great ally to have, especially in times of trouble."

"So what are you going to do with Conde Nast?"

"Carry on running it. I also have to find out if I'll be taking on any other companies. Depends on Vlad's will really. I may approach your firm about installing you on the board. It would be useful to have my eyes and ears on there."

"I'll speak to Mr Carey when I get back to the office. Find out if that's allowed under my contract."

"Otherwise resign, and I'll double the salary they were paying you."

"No!! Ivan, I won't do it. I won't be beholden to you. I've not fully forgiven you for all this, and I need time to recover from it, and the shock I had with my mum, which you seemed to have forgotten about."

"I'm sorry. I've been so caught up in this I've barely thought about much else. Listen, why don't I take you away somewhere nice this weekend? We can relax, play, and put all this behind us."

"I'll give it some thought, and let you know." We were interrupted by a knock on the door. One of Ivan's security team opened it just enough to let the girls in, before closing it again. Bella and Tania raced over to Ivan, and jumped up at him.

"How's my baby girls?" Ivan crooned, "did you miss daddy today? You did? Paws up who wants their tummy rubbed?" Both dogs immediately rolled onto their backs, and presented their rather fat little tummies to Ivan for fuss. He petted them for a few minutes with a tenderness that was at odds with the hardman gangster image of him that I'd built in my head over the previous few days. "You are the prettiest little girls in the world, yes you are," he cooed, as they both wriggled in delight.

"I wish you talked to me like that." I said. Ivan stopped rubbing, and gaped at me.

"You want your tummy rubbed too?"

I sighed, "no, I just wish I was more sure of you. You dropped a bombshell on me yesterday, and it was only a surprise because most of the time you're either barking orders at me, or talking dirty. A bit like when you scared me by telling me we'd have wild sex, rather than just saying you wanted to make love."

"Do I actually get anything right?" He looked annoyed.

"Not lately." A thick silence spread between us. "I'm gonna get back to work. I take it I won't need security anymore?"

"Roger will pick you up. Just call him as you're leaving. Can I see you tonight?"

"I'll let you know." I picked up my handbag and left, heading straight to the office.

Lewis was surprised to see me back. "The job finished early. Their HR director was organised to the point of obsessive. She had it done by nine this morning. Did you see the news this morning?"

"I did indeed. Quite a coincidence isn't it?" Lewis said.

"What? Do you think I stuck pins in a doll or something?"

Lewis laughed, "no, I mean she goes back to Porenski and dies in a car crash. Maybe a jealous ex of hers had his nose out of joint."

"No idea. I did hear that her father had contracts on his head. Do they suspect foul play then?"

"Apparently not. The police statement just says they are performing tests on the driver. Maybe they think he was drunk. Witnesses reported seeing him driving erratically for quite a distance before he lost control and crashed."

"Wonder why they didn't ask him to stop the car then? I would if a driver was that bad." I said. Lewis nodded in agreement. "I'll be in my office if there's anything you need me for." I headed down the corridor. Laura smiled as I walked in. "Any problems?" I asked.

"No, some calls for you to return, but that's all." She handed me a list of callers. "So what was Conde Nast like?"

"Glamorous. All the staff seemed impossibly stylish. The department I was looking at was very well run though. It's why I'm back early."

"Did you know about Ivan's girlfriend?"

"Yes, I was there during his press conference when he found out. The poor man went white."

"I thought it was you he was with, then she popped up. All very confusing."

"Yeah, well, they went back a long way. I couldn't compete really. He was engaged to her at one point."

"He might need you to console him Elle. Get back in there girl." Laura looked so hopeful that I had to laugh.

She went off to make drinks, and I settled at my desk and switched on my screen. I read through the list of calls to return, and straightaway saw Lucy's name. I picked up the phone. "Hi Lucy, you called."

"Yup. Opened those wills. The only person we need to call in is Ivan Porenski. I spoke to the police and hospital regarding the case, and we're assured that the father died first, daughter second. He left everything to her, she left everything to Porenski. Obviously as named executors, we need to ascertain the extent of the assets, and there will be inheritance tax to pay, but Mr Porenski will need to be told as soon as possible."

"I'll contact him and call you back. It may be better for you to come over here, I'll let you know."

"Ooh, I'd love to. See what you can arrange." We said our goodbyes, and I called Ivan.

"Hi. Just had a call from our family law department. They need to speak to you urgently. Can you come to my office this afternoon? Or we come to yours?"

"Yes of course. I can do three, that ok?"

"Yes, fine. My office?"

"Sure." The phone went dead. *Grrr*

I called Lucy straight back, who was delighted with the prospect of an afternoon out. I sat and did some work, emailing my time sheets over to the accounts department for my day and a half at Conde Nast, and replied to some other client queries. At half two, Lucy turned up.

"Wow, your office is quite something," she said, looking around, "and the view is to die for. Bloody wish I'd been clever enough to do corporate. So apart from a swanky office, how's life?"

"Up until last weekend, life's been great. James and I get on fantastic, I love the flat, my jobs busy, and I've been out to some fab places. What about you?"

"Work's fine. Nothing stellar like you though. I split up with Hugo a while back, which I was pleased about, and I've been just dating different people since. Went to Tuscany for a week in May, and moved into a new flat in Chelsea with my brother....what happened last weekend then?"

"My mum died. Found dead on the Sunday morning by her partner. Aneurysm."

"Oh babe, that's terrible. Such a shock for you. Were you very close?"

"Yeah. She was the only family I had. We're a long line of only children, so no cousins, or anything." Lucy looked sympathetic. I changed the subject to ask about the others on our traineeship. Everyone seemed to be doing fine, although we were all working extremely hard.

At three, Ivan appeared. Lucy reacted in the same way I'd seen countless women do. She pinked up, got a touch flustered, and I could almost see her brain short circuit. She stood and held her hand out, unable to take her eyes off him. Ivan smiled thinly, and shook her hand. I introduced them both, and we all sat down. Lucy pulled a folder from her bag. "Now Mr Porenski, we received word that two clients of ours were killed in an accident this morning. We hold their wills, and I have copies of both wills here. I have spoken to both the Metropolitan police, and Hammersmith General hospital to ascertain the circumstances, and am satisfied that the times of death on their certificates, plus witness statements show that Mr Meranov died first, with Miss Meranov, approximately half an hour later on board the air ambulance. Mr Meranov left his entire estate to his daughter, with no exceptions. You are the only beneficiary of Miss Meranov's will, and it is clearly stated that there are no exceptions. Now, Pearson Hardwick have been appointed as executors, and as such, we have to ascertain the assets of Mr Meranov, and Miss Meranov before we can advise the tax authorities of the inheritance tax position, and apply for probate."

Ivan didn't react at all. "You'll find their business interests will all be registered as Russian, and their homes here were owned by their companies. I will send you all the paperwork as soon as I have it translated, and will deal with the notaries in Russia myself. It should all be quite straightforward for you."

Lucy smiled, "Excellent, are there no other assets apart from company ones?"

"Only a day to day bank account each, I don't know how much either would have held, but probably not too much. Vlad kept all his assets in Russia as much as possible as its much safer."

"Safer? How come?" I asked.

"He was a marked man, and he knew it. There is no inheritance tax in Russia between family members, and only 13% to non family. He wouldn't want the British government helping themselves to 40% of his wealth. He spoke about the subject a lot."

"I see. Where did he live?"

"Windsor. They both did. Dascha moved back there in December."

Lucy pulled a business card out of her bag. "Here are my contact details. As soon as you can furnish me with details of their British assets, I can apply for probate. Now if you have any questions at all, please feel free to contact me." *Was she flirting?*

"Thank you. My secretary will be in touch. Now, I need to speak with Elle about a different matter." He looked at Lucy expectantly. She took the hint, and said her goodbyes. "So, are you feeling better?" Ivan inquired.

"I wasn't ill, just upset." I replied warily. "I'm happy to work with you Ivan, but I don't think I want a relationship with you. I just...." I trailed off.

"Just what?" He barked. "Tell me Elle. Tell me what I have to do, because I don't understand you."

I just stood there, trying not to react to his anger at me. I had the inexplicable urge to cry. "Ivan, I'm scared of you. That's the problem. You scare me, and in my work life, I can cope. In my home self, I can't. I'm sorry." A big, stupid tear rolled down my face, betraying me. I swiped it away angrily. I didn't do crying at work. "All I know Ivan, is that you like to fuck me, have me followed, and put my life in danger for a stupid deal. Hardly romance of the year is it?"

"I don't do romance. I would have thought you were far too logical to do it either."

"Maybe not. I can't be with someone I don't trust though. I was convinced you'd sacrifice me during that deal. Now, I know you didn't, but what I'm trying to say is that I thought you would. That's how unsure I am of you. So it's best you find someone else who doesn't care what sort of relationship you have, as long as you buy her a red dress and some rubies."

"So, you want to run back to Oscar? Is that what you're trying to tell me?"

"No, I didn't say that. For all his issues, even Oscar sends flowers. I never doubted his integrity, or that he cared about me."

"Cared enough to get Dascha killed? This has all the hallmarks of a British intelligence hit. Oscar *is* the establishment, he could have done it to keep you safe. Still think he's a man of integrity?" Ivan spat the words out with disdain. I shrugged.

"I have no idea what he did or didn't do, and besides, this isn't about him, it's about you. Your assertion that you were in love with me was a complete shock. Don't you see? I didn't have a fucking clue, because you don't show it. No hearts, no flowers, and you can't even say goodbye on the phone, you just slam it down on me. Now, if you want to go through life not doing romance, that's absolutely fine, just be aware that it won't be with me."

Ivan glared at me with his laser beam eyes. "Fine, if that's how you want it." With that, he stomped out. I sat back in my chair, and tried to compose myself in case any of my colleagues arrived. I was in turmoil inside, the fors and againsts of being with Ivan rattling around my head. He was beautiful, fun and sometimes so nice, yet there was that sinister undercurrent that led me to believe my own paranoia that he would have kidnapped me to stop that deal. I tried to sit and think rationally, but all the stress and worry of the last few days seemed to cloud my head. As it was gone five, I decided to head home, eat, and spend a quiet hour in the gym. Some exercise might help.

I didn't bother to call Roger, as it was a beautiful summers evening, and I wanted to walk. I stopped off at the deli for some basics, and strolled along, lost in thought. The flat was fine. It didn't look as though anyone had tried to break in, and the solitude was a welcome novelty after having 24 hour security with me for the last few days. I made a latte, changed into workout clothes, and put a wash on. I was just about to leave for the gym, when there was a knock at the door. "Who is it?" I called out.

"Ivan." *Oh great he knows the door code now.* I opened the front door to find Ivan carrying an enormous bouquet of flowers. I noted that he looked rather pensive. "Can I come in?"

"Sure. Are those for me?" He nodded, and thrust them at me rather awkwardly. "Thanks, they're lovely"

"I'm sorry."

"For what?" I asked, as I placed the flowers on the island, and ducked down to search for a vase under the sink.

"For being such an arse, for shouting at you, for being so wrapped up in this deal I forgot about your mum. The list is quite endless really."

I nodded, "Would you like a glass of wine?" I didn't want to say that he was forgiven, I needed more from him than a bunch of flowers and a small 'sorry'.

"Please. Are you going to the gym?"

"Just about to. I've not been since last week, and I need to let out some tension."

"Can I come with you? We could work out together. I'm a member at your gym too."

"Ok, sure." *This could be interesting.*

Ivan called someone to bring a gym bag over to mine. "It'll take about 20 minutes. More wine?" I shook my head. I didn't think it was a great idea to drink before a workout. I pulled a bottle of water out of the fridge, and took a swig before offering it to Ivan.

"Is it a good idea to be seen in public with me? After, you know, you're meant to be the heartbroken fiancé."

"I'm pretty heartbroken that you don't want to be with me anymore, so I think it'll be quite convincing should there be nosy press around."

"Hmm, well, it might be quite busy this time of night, so be warned." A knock on the door announced the arrival of his gym kit. *Do they all know the bloody door code?* We headed down to the car.

Every female head turned, and a few male ones too, as Ivan walked into the gym in shorts and a vest. I was already running full pelt on a machine, iPod blasting Alex Clare into my ears. Whether it was the fact that every head in my line of sight turned, or the electricity that hummed through me whenever he entered a room, I don't know, but I felt his presence before I even saw him. He walked over to me, and after a few stretches, started up the treadmill beside me.

I ran for a full twenty minutes, revelling in the feeling of tension release. Eventually I slowed down and stopped. Ivan's guard immediately handed me a bottle of water and my towel. I took a long swig, watching Ivan's muscular body while he ran. He looked like a well oiled machine as his muscles flexed and moved, glistening with sweat. I noticed the surreptitious glances of most of the women in there, amused as they all seemed to want to work out with him in their line of sight. He seemed oblivious.

Seeing that I was done, Ivan slowed down, and stopped, to join me at the weight machines. He followed my workout, simply using heavier weights. We did alternate sets, each watching the other with heated eyes. We finished with a swim race, which as usual, I won. "You, darling girl, are a machine, and it's very, very sexy," Ivan muttered in a low voice.

"I think you got that the wrong way round. Every woman in here has their tongue hanging out, and is holding their knickers up to stop them falling down, especially now that you're publicly single." He looked amused.

"My housekeeper has made us some dinner, unless you'd rather eat out?" I shook my head.

"I could eat a horse right now. I've not eaten since dinner at Oscar's Sunday night." He looked surprised at my revelation.

"How come?"

"Couldn't stop for shopping last night, and too uptight to eat much anyway. I lose my appetite when I'm stressed or upset."

"My housekeeper has made us a goulash. Come and let me feed you. See you outside in ten." With that, he got out of the pool with every set of female eyes in the place following him, and headed into the changing rooms.

I showered quickly, and threw on a track suit before meeting Ivan out front. I didn't even dry my hair, or apply makeup as it seemed every woman in the changing rooms wanted to ask me about him. I had trotted out the line that I was just his lawyer about ten times, before they all slinked away, realising that I wasn't a font of information, nor would I pass on their phone numbers.

Chapter 12

Back at his apartment, Ivan pulled some dishes out of the warming drawer of his oven, and dished up steaming mounds of goulash and rice. He poured two glasses of red wine, and set mine down in front of me at the island. The dogs sat begging at our feet, but he said no to them. Goulash probably wasn't good for dogs.

"I never know what you're thinking," Ivan said suddenly, breaking the silence between us.

"I was thinking that the girls would probably be poorly if they ate what we're having."

"Oh.........I meant about us really. We don't seem to have resolved anything, and you're like a closed book. Sometimes I think you wouldn't care if you never saw me again."

I swallowed a mouthful of food. "That's not the case Ivan, and deep down you know it. I find you abrupt and rather controlling, which can be difficult, but fundamentally it's the lack of softness towards me that was my issue. Most of the time you treat me like a bloke, not a girl. It confuses me. Plus of course, I don't trust you."

He pondered my words in silence.

"But you knew I hadn't cheated on you with Dascha? You trusted me enough to play along?"

"Only because she was a rubbish liar, plus as far as I was aware, it had ended between you and I the moment I saw you on the news with her."

"But you seemed fine..."

"In work mode, of course I was. In private, not so much. I was.....disappointed at being so wrong about you, and convinced myself you only pursued me because I kept saying no. I became a challenge," Ivan looked horrified, "plus of course, Oscar had wanted me."

"Elle, that's not true. I wanted you from the moment I met you. I was angry that Oscar got to you first, but both of us wanted you, and neither of us were willing to give up." He took a deep breath, "I'm in love with you. That's the truth. I need to know how you feel about me, I need to know that this isn't futile." His beautiful face looked anxious. I wanted to throw myself into his arms and kiss his troubled look away, but instead I sat frozen.

"It's not futile Ivan. I have feelings for you, but I need time to recover from this terrible episode. I need to see the softer side of you again."

"Can I take you away this weekend? Somewhere nice, where we can relax, swim, eat, that type of thing."

"That sounds lovely. Where to?"

"I have a villa in the south of France. We can go there Friday, come back Sunday night."

"What about Bella and Tania?"

"They can come. They have passports too. It's a touch hot for them, but they like the pool." I looked down at the two of them wagging their tails, as if they understood what Ivan was saying. "The food is wonderful, the sun will be shining, and it has a great pool. You'll love it."

"I honestly can't wait. Looks like those two can't wait either," I said. Ivan looked down at the dogs and laughed.

"Check your schedule for Friday, and we'll leave from London City. I'll organise the jet." I pulled out my iPhone, and read my schedule.

"I can be away by two, if I can clear it with Lewis."

"I'm booking you from two in that case. I'd rather do that than have you use up your leave. We'll be in France by five. By the way, did you get the results yet from the doctor?"

"Yes. All fine. Did you end up getting tested?"

He wrinkled his nose, "yes. Not the most pleasant experience. That doctor didn't like men much I think, she was rather.....rough in the way she handled 'things'. I'm fine though." I laughed at his obvious distaste at the lady doctor. "What's so funny?"

"You. Did you expect her to say a prayer over your man parts?"

"Well, I expected her to be gentle, and treat them with kindness and respect, not don rubber gloves, and behave as if she had something nasty in her hand. She was rather brutal with the swab."

"Poor boy, well if you're good, I'll make it up to you on Friday."

He looked horrified. "You're making me wait till Friday? That's.....cruel."

"Anticipation is the best bit, I'm sure you said that once, besides, you get to go bareback, surely that's worth waiting for?" I flirted. *Oh you'd better be good between now and Friday, lover boy.*

I went home that night, kissing Ivan goodbye with the promise of seeing him Friday afternoon. The next day I had to hit the ground running to catch up with all my work. I even remembered to call Lady Golding and organise an afternoon in town with her the following Wednesday. Quintessentially managed to get me tickets for Les Miserables, which I thought she would enjoy.

I schmoozed the first author that evening, and managed to get him to sign for a ten thousand pound advance, much to Justine's delight.

Thursday was similar, in that I barely looked up from my screen all day, racing to make my dinner meeting with the second author. I had barely spoken to Ivan, communicating only really via email, and a late night phone call, which had left me heated and horny. I met the second author in a restaurant in Covent Garden. He didn't seem as much of a pushover as the first, and I let him think he was playing hardball, holding out for an advance of fifteen thousand. I made a show of calling Justine to 'convince' her to pay it. He signed up as soon as she said yes. She, of course was delighted. Even with my fees, she felt she had the bargain of the year.

As soon as I got home, Ivan called, alerted, no doubt by Roger after he dropped me off. "Hey baby, you're back nice and early," he purred in his sexiest voice.

"Got it all wrapped up nice and quick, plus I have stuff I need to do here, packing and things. Your day ok?"

"All meetings, mostly rather tedious. Plus I'm impatient to see you tomorrow. My mind is so preoccupied with thoughts of making love to you, that's it's better I don't attempt any complex business."

"Smooth, Ivan, very smooth," I teased.

"I bought you some bikinis today. I had a little time to shop. I hope you like them," he said softly.

"Of course I'll like them if you chose them. That reminds me, I need to get some suntan lotion."

"I have it. Everything you need is there. All you need is your passport, nothing else."

I went quiet for a moment. "Everything? Are you sure? Clothes, makeup, hair stuff?"

"Everything you could possibly need. I promise. Just pack your passport baby."

"Okaaay, you're not going to make me go naked all weekend are you?"

"Now that's a plan...no darling, I just have it all arranged so you don't have to worry. I'll pick you up from your office at two. Remember, just bring your passport."

"Okay, I'll trust you on this."

"Good. See you tomorrow. Sleep well. Night baby." *Yay at last!*

"Night."

With no packing to do, I spent an hour in the bath, exfoliating, shaving, and applying some tan so I wouldn't look pasty in my new bikinis. I contemplated how it would feel to make love with Ivan again, and a shiver of excitement ran up my spine. The awful events of the previous weekend were beginning to fade, and I began to question whether I had actually got Ivan all wrong, and he had in fact been just as trapped as I had felt.

Next morning, I was at my desk by seven thirty, having closed up the flat, and been to the gym. I worked my way methodically through my emails, and cleared up as much paperwork as I could, knowing I wouldn't be able to do any over the weekend. Steve Robbin's flotation was only two weeks away, so I touched base with him, assuring him that Deloitte and Goldings, the bank involved, were on top of everything, prospectus' had been mailed out to the institutional investors, and as there were few companies going public at that time, interest was running high. Personally, I was hopeful of a great result for him, but kept my opinions out of it, not wanting to raise his expectations too much, in case he ended up disappointed.

Thankfully, the morning flew past, and after a final meeting at one, I was back in my office with my screen off by quarter to two. Lewis had already left for the weekend, poking his head round my door to say a cheery goodbye at mid day.

The last fifteen minutes seemed to take forever. I sat at my desk, watching the clock tick slowly round. Nerves at having no clothes with me kicked in, and I wondered if I had done the right thing in trusting Ivan to provide everything I would need. I figured that a bikini and a sundress would be pretty much all I required, so if I had to do emergency shopping at the airport, it wouldn't matter.

Ivan was wearing a grey suit with a crisp white shirt and charcoal grey tie. As per usual, it took a moment to get over his extraordinary beauty. "Hi baby, did your morning drag too?" He gave me a devastating smile, clearly delighted to see me.

"It did indeed, but I've cleared my work, and it's time to play." I winked playfully at him, before grabbing my handbag, and following him out of my office. In the lift on the way down, I felt his hand drift to my bottom, before giving it a playful tweak.

Surrounded by both Ivan's security, and other workers, I couldn't react other than smiling, and looking sideways at him. He caught my eye and grinned, looking so excited that I wanted to laugh. He mouthed the word 'bareback' at me, before flashing his signature smile. I struggle to suppress a giggle, which came out like a sort of snort. Ivan just grinned even more. *Git.*

Once we were in the privacy of the car, he pulled me to him for a kiss, starting soft, almost chaste, before becoming deeper and needier, his hands roaming over my body, reconnecting physically with me. It was almost a shame that we got to the airport, as I was enjoying our closeness. We pulled apart as we arrived, and I looked out of the window to see the two dogs waiting, both wearing pink collars and leads, and flanked by their own security team.

We were whisked through all the checks quickly, and onto a private jet. Bella and Tania both jumped up onto the seats and settled down, as if it was an everyday occurrence. We sat opposite each other, a small polished table between us. I looked around at the luxurious interior. "Is this your plane?" I asked. Ivan just nodded in reply. When all the security guards were strapped into their seats, the doors were closed, and we began to taxi to the runway.

I noticed the Ivan looked a little pale, and was gripping the arms of his seat. "Are you alright?" I asked, frowning at his pained expression.

"I hate flying," he admitted, his voice tight and strained. I reached over and took his hand, pulling it onto the table, and holding it in both of mine.

"Are you like this for the whole flight?" He nodded in reply, looking the picture of misery.

"I know, it's embarrassing, but I've always hated flying. I'll be a bit better when we're actually in the air...until landing that is."

"Lots of people are afraid of flying. Don't be embarrassed." As soon as I said it, he blushed. It was the first time I'd seen him blush over anything, and I thought it was adorable. His hand gripped mine tighter as we began our take off, and I watched as he began to sweat, a film covering his forehead. As the plane got faster and lifted off the ground, Ivan looked as if he was in pain, squeezing my hand so tightly, it was kinda starting to hurt. "And there was me thinking we'd try our first bareback a mile high," I said.

"Sorry baby, no chance of that. I can't walk around on aircraft, let alone do anything else. Thankfully it's quite a short flight. Long haul is like purgatory for me.

As soon as we were airborne, Ivan seemed to relax slightly. I let go of his hand, and unclipped my seatbelt. Bella must have sensed his distress, as she clambered onto his lap, and licked his face. "Yes I know, Daddy's a scaredy cat. Sorry Elle, did I hurt your hand?" I shook my head, smiling at him. "Now, would you like some champagne?"

"Love some, thank you." The attendant brought out an ice bucket, a bottle of Krug, and two glasses. She placed them in front of us, and poured our drinks. "Cheers," I said, raising my glass to Ivan's. To sun, sea and sex."

"I'll drink to that," he said, touching the edge of his glass to mine. I took a long sip of the champagne, and watched as Ivan dipped his finger in his, and let Tania lick it clean. "I know they shouldn't have alcohol, but she loves champagne." He turned to the dogs, "You're just a good time girl aren't you?" He said to Tania in his 'daddy' voice. She wagged her tail happily, her jealousy at Bella being on his lap temporarily assuaged.

The flight to Nice took just under two hours. Ivan was uptight all the way, although I thought he hid it quite well. He told me about the villa, which he had bought about five years ago, and the village it was in, called Saint-John-Cap-Ferrat. I could tell he was excited at showing it to me. He told me he only ever managed two weeks there at a time, and his goal was to be able to spend a whole summer out there one day, when he wasn't so intent on building up his companies.

He tensed as we began our descent into Nice airport, clinging onto my hand as if it was a life raft. He closed his eyes as we touched down, and I could see the sheen of sweat on his upper lip. Even his hands were shaking slightly. When we taxied to a halt, the tension seemed to leave his body. It was an extraordinary transformation from shuddering wreck back to my confident and assured Ivan.

"That wasn't as bad as normal. Maybe because you're with me," he said, smiling widely. I wanted to laugh. If that was him 'not too bad', I wondered what he was like during a storm or turbulence.

A Mercedes ML met us, and we were quickly whisked away. Ivan explained that the villa was only 16 kilometres from the airport, so it wouldn't take us long. He had shed his jacket and tie on the plane, and looked totally relaxed already. The Mercedes was air conditioned, which was a welcome respite from the blazing heat. The dogs sat between us as we drove along the coast road, the Cote D'Azure shimmering beside us, looking unbelievably inviting.

Eventually, we pulled up at a set of gates on the other side of a pretty little town. Our driver wound down the window, and spoke to the guard on duty in what sounded like Russian. He went into a small hut, and the gates swung open. We drove on, through lush gardens, towards a sparkling white and taupe villa perched on the side of the hill. "It's beautiful," I breathed. Ivan smiled at me.

"Glad you like it. I love it here. It's very private, but there are some great places nearby to visit." We stopped outside a large front door, which was already open, with Mrs Ballard waiting to welcome us.

"Jo, I didn't know you'd be here." I was pleased to see her, knowing she would have taken care of the 'no luggage' thing perfectly.

"I've been here a few days getting the place ready for you. Lovely to see you here. I hope you enjoy your stay." She took the two dogs from Ivan, and unclipped their leads. They immediately raced into the house. The entrance hall was extremely grand, with a stone staircase sweeping up in the centre. The walls were painted cream, and the furnishings were modern and stylish. It looked like something out of a interiors magazine. Ivan led me through to the large living area, past uber contemporary sectional sofas, and out to the terrace and pool. As the back of the property was effectively carved into the mountain, the view was stunning. An unbroken view of the sea in front, and the coastal villages to each side. The pool merged with the sea, making it look as though it was all one.

"Infinity pool," said Ivan, as though he was reading my mind, "cool isn't it?"

"Very. This whole place is gorgeous."

"Like you. Come, let's shower." Ivan led me upstairs, and into the master bedroom, which was decorated in shades of white and pale grey. I checked the closet, and Jo had indeed done me proud with some pretty floaty dresses, a selection of bikinis, as well as shorts, vests and tops. There was way more than I needed for just two days. I closed the door, and followed Ivan into the bathroom, only to find Bella and Tania stretched out on the cool stone floor. "Go find Jo," Ivan said to them, shooing them out, "you can't watch daddy shower." Rather reluctantly they sloped off, looking a little disgruntled. Ivan switched on the jets in the wet area.

"You know, I can't actually believe you're here, and about to get naked and wet with me," he purred, "I've thought about nothing else for the past three days." He unzipped my dress, and planted little kisses on my shoulder as he peeled it off me, before unclipping my bra, letting everything fall to the floor. He caressed my breasts briefly before hooking his thumbs into the waistband of my knickers, and sliding them down my legs. I turned to face him, and began to undo the little buttons of his shirt. Impatient, he undid his trousers himself, and kicked his shoes, socks and the rest of his clothes off quickly. Finally we were both gloriously nude.

We stood under the giant shower head, washing the stickiness of the day away together. I shampooed Ivan's hair, and washed him all over, massaging the tension of the flight out of him. As I moved to wash his legs, his erection twitched in front of my face. I caught it between my lips, and swirled my tongue over the taut skin of the tip. Ivan groaned.

"I feel like I'm on a hair trigger Elle, I might not last too long."

"That's fine," I said before turning my attention to his balls, kissing and licking them gently. I glanced up to see Ivan watching me intently, his eyes filled with pure lust. I ran my tongue slowly over the silky smooth shaft of his dick, teasing it by avoiding the sensitive tip.

"Oh god Elle, that feels so good," he gasped. I cupped his balls with the palm of my hand, rubbing my index finger gently and rhythmically over his perineum. At the same time, I took his cock deep into my mouth, and with my other hand holding the shaft, licked and sucked the wide crest. His voice sounded almost panicked as he garbled, "Elle I'm gonna come, baby I'll end up coming in your mouth, Elle, Elle, now," before he spurted hotly into my mouth. I didn't miss a beat, swallowing every drop he could give me. I watched his beautiful face as he came, from the moment of panic about coming in my mouth, to the moment of vulnerability as he let go, and found his release.

He pulled me up onto my feet, and wrapped me in a tight embrace. "That was so damn good it should be illegal. Now, your turn." He grabbed the shampoo and squirted some in his hand, before lathering up my hair, massaging my scalp with his strong hands. I stood under the water to rinse, and he poured some expensively scented shower gel into hands, rubbing them together to create a lather. He washed every inch of my body, caressing and kneading me all over, in a sensual assault. Just his touch alone was enough to make me feel wanton and horny. "I want you on the bed, not standing up in the shower," he muttered. He shut off the shower, and grabbed a large towel. He wrapped it round me, and quickly dried me off, before towelling my hair, and finally, himself.

In the bedroom, he yanked the covers off the bed, and pushed me down onto the mattress, pulling my legs apart. Within seconds, he was kissing and licking me intimately, sucking lightly on my clit. His warm hand stroked its way up my body to tease a nipple, and caress my breast. When he inserted two fingers inside me, I arched off the bed, my orgasm beginning to brew. "Please, I need to feel you inside me," I begged. I wanted to feel his big cock stretching me. He climbed up my body, and carefully nudged inside me.

"Oh god, you feel amazing, it feels so different," he gasped, as he began to move at a deliciously slow pace. He propped himself up on one hand, and with the other, reached between us to play with my clitoris. The combination of his cock rubbing my g spot and his fingers flicking my clit, caused an enormous orgasm that took over my entire body. I cried out as I came, and could only lay helpless as I pulsed around his cock.

He began to pump hard, hammering into me, causing my orgasm to go on and on, making me so horny, that all it took was his hot mouth around my nipple to launch me into another shattering climax. He watched me intently as I came, his laser eyes boring into me, as if he was trying to see inside me. As my orgasm began to subside, he pressed in deep, and let go, giving me a fleeting glimpse of his vulnerability as he poured himself into me.

He collapsed onto his elbows as he recovered, and kissed me deeply, before lifting his head up to gaze into my eyes. "We are so good together, don't you think?" Ivan whispered.

"Definitely," I replied, smiling at him. "So was it different without the condom?"

"Oh god, yeah. I'm spoilt for life now," he said, smiling widely, before pulling out of me. He grabbed some tissues from the bedside table and gently dried me off in an intimate and tender gesture. Satisfied, he lay down beside me, and pulled me into an embrace. His body felt soft and warm, his strong arms, safe and secure as they held me tightly to his chest.

"I will make you love me Elle, I promise," he murmured, "I will be the man you fall in love with. I just hope that you will love me as much as I love you, because I love you with every fibre in my body."

I pondered his words. I felt a closeness to Ivan that I'd never had with anyone else, as if we were kindred spirits. I loved how he made love, seemingly totally in sync with my body, riding my orgasms as though they were his own. I loved his complexity, and his sudden, and unexpected vulnerabilities. *I love him. Bugger.*

"I think I'm in love with you too. It scares me," I blurted out. He pulled away to scan my face.

"Baby, don't ever let it scare you. What we have, we should enjoy. We have to grab this happiness and hold onto it." He smiled tentatively at me. I smiled back, and kissed the tip of his nose. "Now, what do you say we get dressed, and go out to eat? There's the most fabulous little restaurant just on the way to the village."

"That sounds wonderful."

Chapter 13

We drove down to a tiny little restaurant, hidden off a small courtyard. Ivan was relaxed enough to let his security wait outside. The owner was a smiley, and rather rotund Frenchman called Pierre. He seemed to know Ivan quite well, and recommended some dishes that he assured us used the freshest, and best fish from the market that day. We both decided to let him choose, and we were delighted at our fillet en papillote. Ivan was relaxed and chatty during our meal, it seemed as though a great weight had been lifted from him. As we sat and drank our wine. I noticed that Ivan looked thoughtful.

"Elle, what's your ambition in life?"

I thought for a moment, "to make partner in a top law firm. To be comfortably off. Beyond that, I don't really know. What about you?"

"I want to own the world, then lay it all at your feet."

"You seem to own a lot of it already. Do you really need more?"

"Yes," he said without hesitation, "I'm not the richest man in the world."

"Is that your goal?"

"Yes." As he said it, I caught a glimpse of the peasant boy from the slums of Moscow, so scared of returning to that life, he would dedicate the rest of his days to the pursuit of the security of wealth.

"We are both a million miles away from poverty already," I said, "neither of us will ever go back to those terrible times."

"I'm not ashamed of it," he said, "I just don't want to return to it. Sometimes I feel as though I'm not as cultured as the people around me, but I just try and learn as much as I can, so I can fit in."

"I think you're very urbane. I didn't realise you started out a poor immigrant until you told me."

He smiled, "that's kind of you to say. I'm trying to learn about fine wines at the moment, to keep up with Oscar."

"The cellars at Conniscliffe are amazing. It all seems a little pointless though, to own more wine than you could ever possibly drink."

"A valid point, but Oscar is all about legacy. Building for the next generation." I nodded in agreement. "Do you think you'll ever have children?"

"I don't know," I admitted, "I'm afraid to lose or damage my career, it's my fear, ending up like my mum, a single mother, and poor, scraping around to keep a child fed. I would have to be very sure."

Ivan changed the subject. "Shall we head back? I have an inexplicable urge to make wild, passionate love to you again."

"Great, let's go," I said brightly, which made him laugh. He paid the bill, and tipped Pierre generously. As soon as we were in the car, he pulled me onto his lap for a kiss.

"I want to taste you tonight, lick and suck you, until you come on my face," he murmured quietly in his phone sex voice.

"Hmm, sounds good," I whispered, "but I do love it when that big cock of yours makes me come." I could feel him harden underneath me. He groaned.

"How am I going to get out of the car with a big erection?"

I shifted off his lap, "It'll have gone down by the time we get there. Otherwise just carry my clutch in front."

"It's your fault. I feel like a sixteen year old boy again when you're around. It's not funny having uncontrollable erections and an obsession with your tits. I'm a grown man, I should be over such things."

"I'm rather glad you're not. I love how sexual you are, as long as it's aimed at me of course."

"Oh, it's aimed at you, I promise you that. I love how you go from buttoned up lawyer to such a tiger in bed. It's very sexy you know. When I see you at work in your smart suits, toe to toe with the men, you are a different person to when you're wet and naked, with those perky tits rubbing up against me.....fuck, I'm hard again."

I sniggered, "it's all your own fault this time, and we're back at the villa. Here, hold my bag." I handed him my clutch, which he held in front of his trousers as we scuttled to the front door. He made a brief fuss of Bella and Tania, before pulling me upstairs to our room.

"Baby, tell me what you want, what's your deepest desire? I want to make you scream tonight."

"I paused, "I've got no idea, I liked the swing though."

"Can I try something with you? I want you to tell me straightaway if you're not enjoying it though." Ivan's eyes glittered with desire.

"Ok, I'll try." I was so horny for him, I'd give anything a go. Plus I'd liked everything we'd done before.

He closed the bedroom door, and sat on the bed. "Take your clothes off." I stood in front of him, and began to strip slowly, teasing him, giving him glimpses, then turning away. I was only wearing a dress and knickers, so had to work at slowing it down. Eventually I was naked, hot and slick, revelling under his heated gaze. He beckoned me over to him, and I stood directly in front of him. He captured a nipple in his mouth, and sucked hard, causing a spike of pleasure that ran straight to my groin. His hands stroked up my legs, one slipping round to the base of my spine, while the other stroked between my legs. "You're soaked, I really like that." His voice was hoarse. "I want you on all fours on the bed. I won't be a moment."

I did as he requested, moving the covers out of the way. As I perched in position, I wondered where he'd gone, and what he was planning. A shiver of anticipation ran through me. I strained my ears to listen for any clues as to his return, but heard nothing.

Eventually the door opened, and Ivan padded in. I turned to look at him. He was naked, and holding a tray of what looked like sex toys. "Now darling, I think you shouldn't be peeking. I'm going to blindfold you so that you just feel. Now if anything makes you uncomfortable, I want you to say straightaway."

"Ok." He placed the tray down on the bed beside my foot, and kneeled beside me to put the blindfold on. As soon as I couldn't see, all my senses of sound, touch and smell seemed heightened. I jumped slightly as he stroked my behind.

"You are so very lovely Elle, and tonight, I want to possess every inch of you. Would you like that?" He stroked my clit with a featherlight touch as he spoke. I barely managed a garbled noise in reply. I felt the bed dip as he got off, and felt it move behind me.

His tongue on my clitoris made me jump again, before I relaxed into its satin caress. His index finger stroked between my buttocks, rubbing my anus as he worked on my clit. I shivered slightly as his tongue slid upwards to lick the puckered opening where no man had gone before. It felt alien and naughty, but totally erotic and intimate. I felt bereft when he stopped, and shifted slightly, until I felt his cock nudge into me. He held it still for a moment, which puzzled me, until I felt something cool and hard press against my anus. I gasped as he pushed it inside me, in that forbidden place. With his large cock inside me too, I felt overwhelmingly full.

He began to move at a gentle pace, keeping an even rhythm, as I got used to the sensation of having something in my bum. I heard a click and a buzz of a vibrator, before Ivan reached round, and pressed it onto my clitoris, while keeping his steady thrusts. With his other hand, he tweaked and pulled at whatever was in my anus. The surfeit of stimulation was intense, and the orgasm brewing threatened to rip me apart.

"Does that feel good baby?" He purred.

"Hmmmmm yeah, mmmph," I couldn't even speak, I was so overtaken by the sensations in my body.

"Rest your neck on the pillows, and squeeze your nipples for me." I managed to do as he asked, trying to absorb the pleasure building up inside, as every erogenous zone was assaulted.

I actually screamed when I came, feeling as though my entire body was orgasming. Ivan kept up his sensual assault, supporting my body with the arm holding the vibrator as I shook uncontrollably around him. As I came again, he dropped the vibrator, and began to power into me with forceful, and deep thrusts, that wrung every drop of pleasure out of me. As my orgasm subsided, he stilled, and grunted as he came, pressing himself fully inside me.

We both collapsed onto the bed, panting, and slicked with sweat. He pulled off my blindfold before kissing me deeply. I lay boneless in his arms, as he slipped out of me, and removed whatever it was from my bottom. He cleaned me up tenderly, before pulling the covers over me, and getting up to dispose of everything in the bathroom, and open the door for the girls. They raced in, and hopped onto the bed, waiting for Ivan to join us. They immediately snuggled into him, possessively laying between us.

I woke up to bright sunshine streaming in through the large windows looking out to sea. Ivan and the girls were still fast asleep, with Bella so stretched out that I was perched on the very edge of the bed. I swung my legs out, and after brushing my teeth and hair, picked out a bikini, and put a pair of shorts on over the top.

I headed down to the kitchen area, which was one of those glossy, white kitchens that doesn't have door handles. It took me a while to work out how to use the coffee maker, and where to find a mug. Eventually I had a cup of steaming coffee, which I took outside to drink on the terrace. I sat on one of the comfy outdoor sofas while I sipped it, looking out to sea, and watching the yachts in the harbour, just along the bay. It was....perfect.

I sat mulling my perfect life, perfect job, my perfect boyfriend, and this perfect place, and a sob broke free as I thought of my poor mum, who had never been anywhere like this in her life. She had thought that a hundred quid in her knicker drawer made her rich, and had settled for Ray, figuring that any man who didn't hit her was a decent catch. My heart broke for her, and a few tears began to roll down my face.

"Baby what's wrong?" Ivan asked, looking concerned. I'd been so wrapped up in my thoughts, I hadn't noticed him coming outside. "Did I do something to upset you?"

"No, oh definitely not. I was just having a moment over my mum. She never experienced anything like this place. It's just so lovely, and so perfect. I feel so sad for her." Ivan stroked my hair, and bent down to kiss my cheek, before sitting down next to me.

"I still get like that sometimes over my parents. When I bought this place, I sat exactly where you are now, and did the same thing. Cried that they would never experience the things that

I had, that I could never show them this whole other life. My father would have loved it here."

"My mum would have been intimidated, asking nervously if we were 'allowed' to make our own coffee."

"My mum would have washing hanging over the balcony by now, and be wanting to help the staff with the cleaning. She would be horrified at how much I spend on a weekly basis." He smiled as he thought of her.

"You are quite profligate," I mused.

"So what? I make it so that I can live well. No point being one of those rich people who live like paupers and leave it all to the cats home. Plus I'm a nouveau riche Russian, I'm meant to be flashy, it's the law I think." He winked, making me laugh.

"So, what's the agenda for today?"

"Relaxation, maybe a little shopping, some swimming, and lots of sex." Ivan took my coffee out of my hand, and took a gulp, wincing because it didn't have sugar in it.

"Hey, took me half hour to work out how to make that."

"I haven't worked out that coffee maker yet, and Mrs Ballard isn't in for another ten minutes."

I got up, and took the last swig of coffee, "I'll make us both fresh ones." As I busied myself in the kitchen, Jo arrived with a basket of pastries and breads. We chatted easily as she laid a large tray with breakfast things for us. I carried the coffees, and she took the tray, laying it on the low table on the terrace, in front of Ivan. Bella and Tania eyed it covetously.

We had a simple meal of warm, fresh bread, locally made cheese, pastries and fruit, sharing with the dogs. I felt fat and replete. "Come, the suns starting to blaze, we need to cover ourselves in lotion, and I need to cool down in the pool," said Ivan, taking my hand to pull me up. We wandered down to the pool, where lotion, towels, and bottles of iced water were waiting. I slipped off my shorts, and stood while Ivan patiently coated me in sunscreen in long, firm strokes. "You chose the bikini I bought for you," he said, as he moved the straps to the side to make sure I was well covered.

"I really like it. It stood out for me." I took the bottle of sun cream, and coated Ivan, running my hands over his silky, golden skin, feeling his hard muscles underneath. I noted that he even had attractive feet, as I covered him carefully. The two dogs sat under an umbrella, on a padded sunbed, and watched. Ivan made sure their water was cold, before diving gracefully into the pool. I watched in amusement as both spaniels flung themselves in with him, and doggy paddled over. I slid in as well, and Ivan and I played with the dogs, throwing a ball to each other, while the dogs tried to get it. After a little while, they began to tire, and we all retired to the steps at the shallow end, sitting in the water to keep cool.

We were interrupted by Jo bearing a tray of cold fruit for us, and a large frozen lump of something for the dogs. I peered at it, wondering what it was, until she explained that it was chicken stock and water, with toys frozen inside. It would cool them down, and keep them busy for at least an hour. We picked at the icy cold peach and strawberry slices, feeding each other seductively.

"You know I could take you in the pool, nobody would see us," Ivan murmured.

"What about your security?"

"They don't watch me at home, they are all watching the perimeters." His eyes glittered with lust. I hopped into the pool, and took off my bikini bottoms, placing them on the edge.

"What are you waiting for?" I flirted. He flashed his film star smile, and jumped in, swimming underwater to see between my legs. Popping up in front of me, he peeled off his shorts, and placed them on top of my costume.

"I do like it when you're wet and naked," he said, rubbing his body up against mine. He glanced around, before untying the straps of my top, and peeling it off. He caressed my breasts for a moment, playing with my nipples, rolling them between his fingers and thumbs. I reached down to stroke his erection, making him moan. I braced my back against the wall of the pool, and wrapped my legs around his waist. He guided his cock into me, and we began to move.

At first it was a bit splashy and awkward, but we soon found our rhythm, and I leaned back slightly to let his cock bump over my g spot, until I felt the orgasm begin. Ivan continued to play with my nipples, as I reached between us to rub my clit. He gazed into my eyes as I came, not the earth shattering orgasms of our more intense sessions, but a good one all the same. I held him still with my legs as I fluttered and pulsed around him, and felt him swell, and let go, as my climax prompted his.

We clung together for a few minutes, before he kissed me deeply, and pulled out. He popped his head up to scan the terrace, and make sure nobody was around. With the dogs still busy licking their chicken popsicle, we were alone. We stayed in the pool, swimming like naked water babies, enjoying each other's bodies, freed from the confines of ever present staff, and their watchful eyes.

By lunchtime we had covered up, and were laying under the parasols, with the dogs flat out and snoring. Ivan told me about his companies, how he got started, and how he grew them so quickly. We talked about Vlad's companies, what they did, and how Ivan would handle them. He explained some of the Russian company laws, and the conventions of doing business there.

We were talking about the mining laws, when Jo brought out steak and salad for lunch, accompanied by a fruity red wine. We ate in the covered part of the terrace, as the sun was really blazing. "How would you like a spot of shopping this afternoon?" Ivan said, "it's siesta now, but we could go about five, have a look around, see if there's anything we like."

"That sounds like fun."

I headed up for a shower around four, and put on a cute little floaty dress I found in the closet. Jo had done a magnificent job of stocking the bathroom with all my favourite products. I did my hair, applied a touch of makeup, and found a pair of bright blue flip flops to match the dress.

Ivan looked edible as he emerged in a pair of denim cut offs, and a loose, linen shirt. He had a touch of dark stubble, and his hair was left curly and a bit messy. He tucked his wallet in his pocket, and we set off.

Saint-John-Cap-Ferrat was a pretty little town, full of quaint little shops, and charming cafes. Ivan kept his arm round my waist as we meandered around, looking in shop windows, with Nico, and a guard I didn't know, trailing along behind.

We looked in antique shops, boutiques, and salons of modern art, before Ivan stopped us outside a jewellers, to look in the window. "That necklace would look lovely on you," he said, pointing to a dainty diamond and gold filigree piece displayed on a black jeweller's bust.

"It's beautiful," I agreed. I didn't particularly want him to buy it for me though, as I still had the ruby set, albeit left at his Sussex house.

"Come and try it on. I want to see what it looks like on your lovely neck." We wandered into the shop, and Nico translated for Ivan. Russian into French, so I didn't have a clue what they were saying. The woman in the shop unlocked the window display, and took out the necklace, handing it to Ivan to look at. He turned it over in his hands, examining it, before placing it around my neck, and doing up the clasp. He turned me to look at me, assessing the total effect with his sharp, sapphire eyes. "Beautiful," he breathed, "I'll take it."

"You don't need to, I wasn't expecting anything," I said, concerned that he may have felt obliged to buy me a gift.

"Which is why I want you to have it. It's a beautiful piece, and it does you justice," he said, smiling at my frowning face. "Indulge me. Please."

"Thank you, it's beautiful, I love it." I leaned up to kiss him. He looked pleased.

I kept the necklace on as we wandered through the little streets, looking in shop windows. I bought Ivan a little pair of gold cufflinks with a pretty, enamelled shield on them, which he loved. "That's the first gift I've been given in about fifteen years," he said, his eyes shining with some sort of emotion.

"No! Surely other girlfriends have bought you things?" I didn't want to say Dascha's name, but that was who I meant.

"No. Too busy buying themselves stuff. I don't think she ever even got me a birthday present. Would have gone crazy if I'd forgotten hers though." He was clearly talking about Dascha. My heart broke a little bit for him, and I vowed to always buy him nice birthday and Christmas gifts, if we stayed together.

We stumbled upon a tiny cafe, with outside tables, so decided to sit and have a coffee, and watch the world go by. I sipped my latte, and watched the holiday makers, with their happy children, carrying beach bags back to their hotels and guest houses. The little streets seemed to fill with people, some dressed for their evening out, others still in their shorts and sarongs. Youths rode around on little scooters, wrapped up in their own lives. It felt like I was a million miles away from London, and I actually rather liked it.

"What are you thinking?" Ivan asked.

"Just how lovely this place is, and how far away we are from Canary Wharf, but it's nice."

"You could come here for your holiday. We could both take a fortnight off."

"I'm off for two weeks in a fortnights time. I'm going to Spain with my flatmate. It's already booked."

"I see." His lips flattened into a thin, rather grumpy, line. "I'm not sure about you going away with another man."

"I can't let him down now. That wouldn't be fair." I thought of James' disappointed face if I told him I wasn't going. I couldn't do that to him. "He's my good friend, and I wouldn't do that to him. If I'd known then that I'd be in a relationship with you, I wouldn't have asked him to book it."

"Hmm, do you think he'll try it on with you?"

"Don't be daft, I've been living with him for months. He treats me like his kid sister. Just because you can't keep your hands off me, doesn't mean every man feels the same way you know." He didn't look convinced. "Would you feel the same way if it was Lucy I was going on holiday with?"

"No. Unless Lucy was gay, no, I wouldn't object, but I would assign you some security." Ivan sounded petulant.

"Ivan, this was all organised before we got together, and I'm not going to back out of it, and let my friend down, just because you're snippy about it. We can go away together another time."

"How would you feel if I went away with another woman?"

"If you were here alone with Mrs Ballard, I wouldn't give it a thought. If you went away with a leggy blonde, I'd be concerned. You didn't freak out when I stayed at Oscar's house the weekend."

"I did freak out about you staying at Conniscliffe. It was pure torture, but it was the only way of keeping you safe. I barely slept all weekend, worrying you'd go back to him, and it would have been all my own fault for telling Dascha how I felt about you." He reached over and grasped my hand.

"You really don't need to worry about James. He's a good friend, and I've never had any inkling that he fancies me. If I wanted someone else, I wouldn't be with you. I would end it with you, rather than cheat on you."

"A woman of integrity, a rare and exquisite thing." Ivan smiled at me, the tension broken. "Now, I know a great restaurant on the seafront. Shall we eat there this evening?" He nodded at Nico to go and pay for our coffees.

"Sounds good."

The restaurant was busy and buzzy, and the food exquisite. We had a duck pate to start, and I had lamb for my main. Ivan chose the steak. Everything was precisely cooked, and looked like a work of art on the plate. The red wine Ivan chose went beautifully. I complimented him on his choice, which seemed to please him. It was nearly midnight by the time we got back to the villa, both of us replete and a bit sleepy.

Ivan made love to me slowly, more as a way of keeping our connection than trying to induce a screaming orgasm. It was relaxed, and sensual, holding each other close, enjoying the skin to skin contact. I was relieved not to perform sexual somersaults, given the amount we had both eaten that evening. Instead, it felt simple, loving, and intimate.

The dogs were let in afterwards, and settled themselves down, before we all drifted off to sleep.

Chapter 14

I was still up early, even though it was Sunday. I went downstairs to make coffee, leaving Ivan, and the dogs, fast asleep. Outside on the terrace, it promised to be another perfect day. I had barely sipped my drink, when the two girls appeared, closely followed by Ivan. "I thought we'd take them for a walk along the beach this morning," he said, causing the two dogs to wag their tails wildly. "Would you mind making me a coffee first though? I can't work that machine."

I made him a cup, and brought it out to him. "What time do we have to leave today?"

"Not till around two. Gives us time for some lunch before we head back."

The beach was fairly quiet as it was still early. A few people were setting out sun loungers and parasols, but it was too early for all but a few German hardcore sun worshipers. We strolled hand in hand along the shoreline, the girls dancing in and out of the sea. Even our guards hung back, seeing no danger around, and giving us some privacy. We both walked barefoot, the cool, damp sand scrunching up between my toes, reminding me there was more to life than emails and writs.

Ivan talked about a trip he would have to make to Russia soon, to sort out Vlad's affairs, and see what needed to be done with the companies involved. I was listening intently, but out of the corner of my eye, I saw a movement.

I turned to see Bella doggy paddling out to sea, quite a way out for a small dog. Having seen how quickly she had tired in the pool the day before, I figured it wouldn't be long before she got into trouble. I reacted quickly, throwing down my flip flops and handbag, and dashing into the sea. As soon as the water was deep enough, I kicked off the bottom, and swam towards her as fast as I possibly could.

As I powered towards her, I could see her begin to slip under the small waves, struggling to keep her face out of the water. I was only a few metres away, when she disappeared under the sea. I dived down, to see her little body sinking slowly. I grabbed hold, and powered us back to the surface.

She was unconscious as I trod water, placing her over my shoulder. I rubbed her back hard, which caused her to throw up. Remembering my old life saving classes at Crooklog pool, I turned on my back, cradling her body with mine, and held her little head out of the water as I swam one handed back to shore.

Ivan helped us out of the water, laying Bella down on the sand, where she promptly threw up a load of salt water, spluttered, and tried to stand up on rather wobbly little legs. I noticed that Tania was on a lead, and held by the guard, probably to stop her going in after us.

"Call a vet to meet us back at the house," he barked at Nico, who looked panicked. Nico pulled his phone out, and scrolled through some numbers, before calling someone, and speaking rapidly in French. "Go get the car," he shouted at the other guard. I noticed that Ivan was shaking.

Bella seemed to recover slightly, standing up to try and rid her lungs and stomach of the salt water, before flopping back down on the sand. "I didn't even see what happened until you were halfway out to her," Ivan said. "When she disappeared, I thought I'd lost her."

"I just reacted. If I'd have been a few seconds later, she would have gone. I'm sure she'll be alright though." Tania was straining at her lead to come over and check that Bella was ok. Nico brought her over, and she sniffed Bella over from head to toe. I stood there, dripping, watching them.

Ivan picked up the spaniel, and tenderly carried her to the car. Nico got a couple of towels out of the boot to cover the seat, and I hopped in. Ivan got in, cradling Bella in his lap, and we headed home.

Bella managed to throw up all over Ivan's shirt twice during the short journey. He didn't seem to even notice, let alone care. He carried her into the house, and laid her on the sofa, while he poured her a bowl of water, and waited for the vet. I went upstairs, and changed into dry clothes.

When I came down, a grey haired man was examining her, listening to her chest with a stethoscope. He spoke in French to Nico, who translated into Russian for Ivan. As I had no idea what they were saying, I just sat and rubbed Tania's ears.

The vet looked at Bella's gums, before saying something else, then shaking Ivan's hand, and smiling as he said 'au revoir'. "How is she?" I asked.

"A bit nauseous from all the salt water, but should make a complete recovery. Thankfully you got there just in time." He stroked her head absentmindedly, and I noticed her tail start to wag. I nodded to Ivan to look. "Well, it looks like you're feeling better, silly girl," he said in his daddy voice. The wagging got stronger.

Jo brought us over some coffees. "What happened?"

"Bella decided to swim out to sea, and Elle saw it just in time, and got to her just as she went under," Ivan said, "it's lucky that Elle's such a good swimmer. Nobody else could have got to her that quick. As it is, she swallowed quite a bit of the med, and is probably feeling a little sick."

"Poor baby girl," Jo cooed, rubbing her damp fur. "That was a very silly thing to do." She turned to Ivan, "bet it scared the life out of you."

"I'm still shaking. I really thought I'd lost her." He shuddered at the thought. "Elle, I can't ever thank you enough. You definitely saved her life." He took a sip of coffee.

Bella sat with us on the terrace as we had lunch, managing to keep down some little pieces of chicken, while Tania sulked at not being centre of attention. Ivan seemed quiet and subdued, which I put down to the scare he'd had earlier. "You ok baby?" I asked him.

"Yeah, although I'm angry that security weren't watching. They're meant to prevent this sort of thing happening."

"Accidents happen. She was very quick. Let's just be thankful there's no lasting damage, and anyway, I doubt if the guards wearing suits would have been able to get to her as fast as I could, so please don't blame them for this."

"Yeah, you're right. I need a shower before we leave. I'm all sweaty."

"I need to wash this salt out of my hair, otherwise it'll feel like straw." We finished our lunch, and left Bella in Jo's capable hands while we headed into the large wet room.

I felt Ivan relax as I washed his hair, and massaged his back with the soap. I could feel the knots of tension in his muscles. I washed him all over, then, as he rinsed, I shampooed my hair, and washed the salt off my skin. He seemed in a world of his own, and didn't make a move to even touch me.

I dried my hair, and dressed in the nicest sundress there, so that I could wear it back home, and grabbed my bag, passport, and my new necklace. Back downstairs, Ivan was clipping the leads onto the girls, and speaking in Russian to Nico. He turned to me. "Ready?" I nodded. "Let's go."

The journey home was much like the journey out. Ivan was frozen to his seat, holding my hand tightly for most of the way. The girls seemed subdued too, although I put that down to Bella still being a bit green around the gills, and Tania being attuned to both her and Ivan's moods.

I asked Ivan to drop me off at my flat so that I could get ready for the week ahead, in truth, he seemed to be in a bit of a mood over the mornings events, and a few hours alone was quite appealing. In the end, he acquiesced quite gracefully, and Nico did a brief sweep of the flat while I thanked Ivan profusely for a wonderful weekend. When Nico had given it the all clear, I headed in, and relaxed.

I checked my emails, put a wash on, and nipped round to the mart for a few bits. Back at the flat, I was sweeping the floors when there was a knock at the door. I called out to ask who it was. "Oscar," he called back. I opened up, and invited him in. "You look brown," he said, frowning.

"Been to France this weekend. How come you're not in Sussex?"

"Had a function up here last night. Did you go to Ivan's place?" I nodded "does that mean you're back with him?"

"Yes, I'm seeing him again."

"Are you mad? He put you in terrible danger, and he'll do it again."

"Dascha put me in danger, not Ivan."

"I don't care who it was. You should be running as far as possible from him. What I don't get about you Elle, is I make one mistake, and you tell me it's irrevocable. Ivan puts your life in danger, and you say 'never mind', and jump into bed with him. I just don't get it."

"Oscar, I really think you should mind your own business. Who I'm with has nothing to do with you. You kept me safe from Dascha last weekend, and I'm very grateful, but I did tell you from the outset I wouldn't be coming back to you. Please accept that."

"I just think you can do better than him. I know he's wealthy, but there's issues in his background that are less than savoury. Don't you ever wonder why he won't go anywhere without a posse of bodyguards? I'm far wealthier, yet I don't need them. Elle, you're going to end up living in fear if you stay with him. I don't even care if you go out with someone else, I just want more for you than he can give you."

"I really don't need a lecture from you, thank you. I have no idea how Ivan and I will pan out, it may just be a flash in the pan, or something deeper, I don't know yet, it's very early days. Right now, I'd quite like to be a single girl again, the amount of bloody hassle both of you have caused." I looked him in the eye, "and you both seem to forget that I earned my own living, and supported myself just fine before either of you turned up." He looked chastened. "Oscar, I appreciate you as a good friend, but I can't unsee the image of you and Darius together. I'm sorry, I tried to get over it last weekend, but I couldn't. Now I'm fully aware that Ivan has his faults, believe me, but he's kind to me, and we have a lot in common, so I'm gonna see where it goes. If you can't accept that, then it's your problem."

"Well, when it all goes wrong..."

"Yeah, you can say 'I told you so'. Fine. Just remember, neither of you have treated me particularly well by my standards, so I don't exactly think you should be standing there criticising anybody."

He looked embarrassed. "Don't you think I know that? And I'm trying to make up for it?"

His statement knocked the wind out of my sails a bit. "I don't want to fight with you. By the way, what did you come round for?"

"Nothing really, well, Sunday night telly really. I was a bit bored and a bit lonely."

"There's a bottle of wine in the fridge. Corkscrew's in the drawer. I'm just gonna finish the floor, and I'll join you for top gear."

"Ok." Oscar busied himself with the wine, although I'm sure he winced at the label. I finished sweeping through the lounge, before tidying the cleaning equipment away, and flopping onto the sofa and taking a swig.

We sat in companionable silence for a while watching our program. I was a bit cross at Oscar's outburst, and inside there was a little part of me that thought he might be right. I was also unsure as to why Ivan had turned so arctic on me after I had rescued his dog. Oscar interrupted my musings, "when's your flatmate back?"

"Twelfth of July. We're off to Spain on the fourteenth for a holiday."

"Ivan ok about that?"

"Not really, but it was booked ages ago, so there's nothing he can do. I'm not letting James down."

"Why would you go with your flatmate when you could go with your boyfriend?" Oscar looked puzzled.

"Because I can relax with James, I don't have to be alert and on best behaviour. I can drink too much, eat too much and read books without having to make conversation. Plus he makes me laugh a lot."

"Maybe he's the one you should go out with." Oscar looked a bit pissy.

"I don't even remotely fancy him. It's a shame, because personality wise, we get along fantastic, but there's no sexual tension there. I couldn't imagine shagging him." Oscar seemed to brighten up as soon as I said it. "So who are you seeing these days?"

"Nobody at the moment."

I didn't reply. Instead, I got out the ironing board, and switched on the iron. Oscar looked a little surprised, but it was part of my Sunday night routine to get myself ready for the week ahead. He watched, rather fascinated, as I worked my way through the pile of clothes. "Don't you have someone to do all that for you?"

I gave him a 'don't be daft' look. "It doesn't take long. I only really have to press work tops. My suits go the cleaners, and gym gear doesn't need ironing. Next week is busy, so I like to be organised at the start, in case I don't get a chance." I hung the final blouse on a hanger, and switched off the iron, leaving it on the island to cool down. "I'm gonna need to go to bed in a minute, so I'm going to have to send you home."

"Ok. Maybe we could have lunch in the week?"

"Sure. I'll call you tomorrow when I know my schedule. I know Wednesdays out, because I'm meeting your mum, and Friday, I have the funeral."

I saw him to the door, and said goodnight. When he'd gone, I wondered exactly what he'd wanted. Oscar didn't strike me as the type to want to just hang out, and watch telly. I also wondered why Ivan hadn't called.

I hit the ground running next morning, getting into work by half seven. My schedule told me I had several meetings planned, so I needed to prepare. I also needed to bill Justine for my time and expenses in getting her the two authors signed up, and do some work on the factory purchase for the rotund businessman who had eaten the Italian restaurant out of house and home.

I switched on my screen, and checked my emails, expecting to see one from Ivan. Instead, there were just a few work ones, one from the undertaker, and a load of internal memos, two of which, reminding me that I had to attend the annual law society awards dinner on the thirteenth of July. The night before my holiday. Not ideal when I was flying out at ten the next morning.

I replied, asking for two tickets. I knew it was one of those events that I had to show my face at, and as I already had a choice of lovely dresses, it would only mean a nice appointment with Guiseppe and Andre. I made a note to ask Laura to book me a slot with them.

I returned from my ten o'clock meeting with Mr Carey, to find an email from Ivan.

From: Ivan Porenski
Date: 24 June 2013
To: Elle Reynolds
Subject: Sorry

Darling Elle

I'm sorry if I made you uncomfortable yesterday afternoon, but I was shaken up by the events of that morning. Anything that reminds me of the fragility of the lives of those I love causes me intense pain. I'm sorry I took that out on you. Bella is now back to her normal, rather badly behaved self, and says thank you for saving her, even though it should have been me that saw the danger she was in. I feel bad about that, and I hope you don't think badly of me because of it.

I have meetings today, and I have to fly out to Russia for a few days tomorrow, so can I see you tonight? I can organise dinner at my place.

Love
Ivan xx

I read his email several times, and thought long and hard before replying.

From: Elle Reynolds
Date: 24 June 2013
To: Ivan Porenski
Subject: Re Sorry

Ivan

Glad Bella is recovered, and as I said at the time, it was an accident, and I don't in any way think less of you just because you didn't see it. Tonight would be great, as I've not stopped so far today, and the thought of not having to shop and cook is lovely. Can Roger pick me up from my flat at around 7 please?

Bit concerned about your trip. Make sure you have plenty of security. I will worry about you.

Lots of love

Elle xxx

Within thirty seconds, a reply pinged into my inbox.

From: Ivan Porenski
Date: 24 June 2013
To: Elle Reynolds
Subject: Re Re Sorry

Elle,

I promise I worry more about you. I will have a full team with me, and there are no known or direct threats. I will make sure I'm back by Friday morning at the latest to accompany you to the funeral.

I have to go, I have lots of meetings to get through today. Will tell you all about it tonight. Will see you at seven.

Love
Ivan xx

I read his email, a bit concerned that he had assumed I'd want him at mum's funeral. In one way, I quite wanted the support, but in another, I didn't want to expose him to some of the less savoury people who inhabited my past. I decided to speak to him later about the subject, and went back to the rather tedious matter of the factory purchase.

My workload was so heavy, that I didn't even stop for lunch. Laura brought in a bagel and a latte, which I scoffed at my desk while working. With an afternoon off booked on Wednesday, and the day off on Friday, I was scrabbling to fit everything in. In some ways, Ivan being away would be helpful, as it meant I'd be able to work late without having to explain or justify myself.

I had an afternoon of interruptions, people wanting information or direction on the work we were doing for the clients that I looked after. I finally managed to get away at half six, practically running home, to fling myself in the shower and get changed ready to be picked up.

Ivan enveloped me in a hug as soon as I arrived at his apartment, kissing me deeply. I ran my fingers through his soft, rather messy, dark hair, pulling him to me, and prolonging our kiss. Eventually, I pulled away, needing to come up for air. Ivan looked serious.

"Baby, I'm sorry about yesterday."

"You already said that in your email. Really, don't worry. Nice to see that Bella's back to normal." She wagged her tail, clearly pleased to see me. We went through to the kitchen where I perched on a stool at the island, as Ivan poured two glasses of wine. "So how was your day?" I asked, as I made a fuss of the two dogs.

"Busy, but productive. I met with your boss today to clear up some matters," he said rather cryptically.

"Lewis?" I frowned. I had seen him around quite a bit that day, and he hadn't mentioned meeting Ivan.

"No, Ms Pearson. I had some of my personal stuff to take care of, and I wanted to ask about putting you on the board as a non exec director."

"Oh? What did she say to that?" I had meant to check my employment contract, but as Ivan hadn't mentioned it again, I hadn't bothered.

"She thought it was a great idea, especially if it means you deliver Conde Nast as a client. It will mean attending one board meeting per month."

"Ok. As long as she's in agreement, then that's fine."

"Good, because I'm also making you a non exec at Retinski too. That one is probably a little more involved, but it's a great opportunity for you. It also made your boss a little more relaxed that the use of Pearson Hardwick would be a long term relationship."

"I see. That makes me an employee of yours though."

"Not really, in fact, it almost makes me an employee of yours as I'm managing director."

"Hmm. How do you think the other directors will feel about this?"

"Fine. Ranenkiov thinks you're great, and is happy to endorse you to the rest of the board, and we don't have a lawyer present at the moment, so it's a great opportunity to bring you in. Duchovy, retired in April, and he not only sat on the board, but also headed up the in house legal team. There was no natural successor until you, so it all fits. With Conde Nast, they don't get a say in it. You will be my representative. If they have any sense, they'll welcome you with open arms."

"Will you have to pay my company for this?"

"No. I made an agreement with Ms Pearson to pay you direct. From her perspective it brings in a new client, plus it's extremely prestigious for your company."

"How much will I be paid? And how much work will be required of me?" I didn't have too many spare hours in a day to commit to another job.

"Conde Nast one day per month, plus a few odd days here and there. You'll get 90 thousand a year for that one. Retinski will be nearer two days per month, plus a few odd days as well. You will be paid 250 thousand per year for it."

I thought about it for a nanosecond. "Ok, where do I sign?" Ivan grinned and pulled out two, thankfully short, contracts. I read through them while he dished up salmon and new potatoes. By the time we had finished dinner, I'd read through both contracts, but spotted an issue I needed to clear up.

"There's a clause here that states in the event of anything happening to you, that I assume the role of managing director of Retinski, and chairman of Conde Nast."

"Yes, it's one of those 'just in case' provisions. It's so that none of the companies are left in limbo while my estate is sorted out."

"I see, well that makes sense, although I would have thought the other directors have far more experience than me."

"They don't have your integrity, that's far more important. The others can guide you."

I finished reading, and with Ivan's explanation, decided I was happy to sign. "So tell me about this trip to Russia? I mean, is it safe for you to go there?"

He looked a little pensive, "it's fairly safe, well, as safe as a wealthy man can be. I need to visit a notary and claim Vlad's assets under his will, see the mines, and how they work, grease some palms, and hurry home to you."

"Can't you send a representative?"

"Not really. The notary wouldn't accept it. Plus I need to see the mining operations in person. I couldn't afford to show any weakness or nerves. As I said, I'll have a big team around me, so I'll be well protected."

"Good. I'll be worrying about you all the time you're away." Ivan produced a biro, and we both signed two copies of each contract. I tucked my copies into my handbag. "Does this mean I shouldn't sleep with the staff?" I asked coquettishly.

"I think it's positively encouraged," he flirted, that lovely lustful look in his eyes. He hopped off his stool, and came round the island to stand between my legs, and wrap his arms around my waist. "Stay the night? I won't see you till Friday."

"I was hoping you'd ask," I replied, kissing him.

"Pleasure room?"

"Oh yes please."

Chapter 15

We raced up to the pleasure room, Ivan dragging me by the hand. I was eager to find out what he would come up with, and was already feeling hot and turned on. We barely made it into the room before he was dragging my vest top over my head, and unclipping my bra. He practically ripped off my jeans and knickers, then stood back to look at me, standing gloriously naked, while he quickly shed his T-shirt and shorts. "I want to fuck you really hard and fast against the wall first," he whispered, "then I'll be able to fuck you for three orgasms, in any way you like." I practically came on the spot, just from his phone sex voice, and the sight of his large erection. He slipped his hand between my legs, inserting a finger. "I think you're wet for me already." He pulled his finger out, and sucked my juices off it. "You taste so good, better than fine wine."

He led me over to the wall, and lifted me up, bracing my back against the cool plaster. I wrapped my legs around his hips, and he guided his cock into me. Then he began to move. Oh god, did he move, drilling into me hard and fast, his pubic bone battered my clitoris repeatedly. It was hard, primal sex, his sheer physical power evident as he hammered into me, chasing his orgasm.

I could feel the muscles in his back ripple and strain as he moved, his face determined and full of lust as his sapphire eyes glittered, gazing into mine. He gripped my thighs, hooking my legs over his arms to open my legs further apart. I looked down to see his cock sliding in and out, and it pushed me over the edge. I cried out as I came, my insides contracting viciously, making me want to close my legs to control the pleasure. He held me firm, as I shook and pulsed around him, while he drove into me relentlessly.

Finally he let go, and I watched his face as he came, his beautiful features momentarily screwed up in concentration, then softened as I felt his cock twitch and throb inside me. He kissed me deeply, a needy, intrusive kiss, as though he wanted to be inside me in every way possible.

He lifted me onto the bed, and flopped down beside me to catch his breath. "You weren't meant to come then," he said, smiling at me, "it was meant to get me ready for a longer session."

"Sorry," I said sarcastically, "blame that big cock of yours, it was his fault." His grin got bigger.

"You are so sexy, I just feel hornier for having fucked you. Once is never enough with you." His finger began to trace around my breast, leaving little trails of heat. I drank in the sight of him naked, his silky, golden skin, muscular, powerful body, and his cock, laying thick and heavy, even after an explosive orgasm.

"So what would you like to do to me?"

"I want to watch you fuck me," he purred, "I want to see you ride my cock until you come all over me, then I'm gonna take you from behind with the butt plug in, and then I'll finish you off with a vibrator on your clit while I fuck you again. How does that sound?" *Try tiring.*

"Interesting. Do you want a butt plug while I fuck you?"

"Oh Elle, you're getting brave. I like them, if you're ok with that." He wandered over to the cabinet, and got out a selection of toys, and a bottle of lube. "This one is better for a man, as it vibrates," he said, showing me what looked like a tiny vibrator, "just make sure it's well lubed before you slide it in. Switch it on once it's in me."

I took the bottle of lube, and carefully squirted some on the plug, before Ivan lay on his back, and lifted his legs to allow me access. It felt incredibly intimate, doing that to him. Once it was inserted, I clicked the end round, to hear a faint buzzing. "Ahh, that feels so good," purred Ivan, pulling me to him. I licked my way up his balls, and the shaft of his cock, before lightly sucking the tip, prompting a soft groan.

He cupped my face, to pull me off, and I straddled him, sinking slowly onto his cock, impaling myself on him. I moved slowly at first, trying to make it last, but his dick was iron hard, and the crest was rubbing my spot mercilessly. His warm hands caressed my breasts, rolling and pinching my nipples, sending waves of sensations through my body. I had to speed up, until I was almost bouncing up and down on him, fierce in my need to climax. With no pressure on my clit, my orgasm was going to be a deep, soul shaking one. I leaned back slightly to increase the pressure, at the same time that he pinched my nipples, and I fell into the deepest, most intense orgasm of my life.

I practically blacked out with the intensity. It felt as though my entire body was coming. Wave after wave running through me, focused on the connection between us.

"Oh baby I can feel you coming so hard," Ivan purred, watching me as I shuddered and shook, soaking him.

As my orgasm subsided, Ivan moved me off him, and onto my front, pulling my hips up. In my orgasmic stupor, I barely felt him insert the butt plug, before his iron cock plunged inside me again. He moved slowly at first, wringing the last of my orgasm out of me, before reaching round to press a vibrator to my clit.

He tweaked at the plug, pulling it out, and sliding it back in, as he fucked me. The alien, but erotic sensation taking over my senses, promising an orgasm that would tear me apart.

"Come on baby, let go, I need you to come," he gasped, as he began to thrust into me hard and fast.

I screamed as I came. It was one of those orgasms that rips through your body like a wildfire, consuming every nerve ending in its path. Ivan came at the same time, shouting 'oh god, oh god', as he stilled and pressed into me. I could feel his body shaking, as he slumped slightly onto my back, pushing me flat onto the mattress. I could feel his heart hammering in his chest, and heard the faint buzzing of his butt plug, before he pulled it out and switched it off.

He rolled off me, and flopped onto his back, pulling me into an embrace. I snuggled into his warm arms, and breathed in the heady scent of Ivan and sex. My post orgasmic haze was broken by Ivan yelling "how the hell did you get in here?" I looked over to see the two spaniels sitting about two feet away from the end of the bed, gazing at us.

"You are the nosiest, most disobedient little girls in the world." He turned to me, "I wonder how long they've been watching, the little pair of perverts."

I giggled, "I'm glad we didn't notice them at the crucial point. That would've put you off your stroke." He smiled, and pulled me back into his arms for another kiss.

The moment was broken by the dogs jumping on the pleasure bed, Tania checking Ivan possessively, while Bella, rather disgustingly, began to lick the damp patch on the bed. "Bella, where are your manners?" Ivan said, looking embarrassed.

We decided to go and get into Ivan's bed, as we were both undressed, and it was already half nine. He switched the telly on, and the two dogs snuggled down. I nuzzled into his chest as we watched TV in companionable silence for a while. "What time are you leaving tomorrow?" I asked.

"Around eleven."

"I'm going to be nervous until you get back."

"I go every couple of months. There's nothing to worry about."

"What if something happens to you?"

"Then you'll look after the companies just fine. I know you will."

"Can't you have a tracking device implanted, just in case?"

He laughed, "you really are nervous aren't you? I'll be back before you know it, all grouchy with jet lag, and you'll wish I'd stayed there a bit longer."

"I doubt that very much. I'll be a bag of nerves until you get back."

"What time's the funeral Friday?"

"Midday. You don't have to come if you've only just arrived back."

"I want to support you that day. You'll need it."

"I'll be leaving home around ten. I have to get to Welling, and greet people at the flat, before the hearses leave for the crematorium."

"No problem. I will be back here by seven. I'm flying overnight," he paused, "I have Dascha and Vlad's funerals next week. I don't expect you to attend with me."

"Probably not wise for me to go. There's bound to be press around." I replied, just before I drifted off to sleep, safe and secure in his arms.

I skipped the gym, wanting to spend as much time as possible with Ivan before I had to leave for work. We showered together, and had some breakfast, before it was time for me to go. "Come home safely," I said, not wanting to let him go. For some reason, the thought of not seeing him for a few days was making me feel bereft.

"I'll be back before you know it," he replied, as he pulled me into his arms for a passionate kiss. Roger took me home to get changed, and then dropped me at work. I switched on my screen, and buried myself in the tasks at hand, determined not to spend the next three days moping.

I worked right through till ten that night, pausing only to eat at my desk. I did a phenomenal amount of work, and felt better about taking the afternoon off the next day with my paperwork up to date. I headed back to the flat, and pretty much went straight to bed, exhausted.

The following morning, I hit the gym with a vengeance, getting there the moment it opened. After a fast paced, and gruelling hour, I showered, and did my hair and makeup carefully, knowing that Lady Golding would, of course, be immaculate. I had decided on one of the Roland Mouret dresses, and teamed it with matching heels and my Chloe bag. As I looked in the mirror, I decided that I looked polished enough for her world, even if I didn't feel it. I threw my workout gear into my gym bag, and headed up to my office.

I made a cup of tea, and settled into my chair, switching on my screen. As I waited for it to boot up, I wondered how Ivan was getting on. My tummy flipped, as I saw an email from him in my inbox.

From: Ivan Porenski
Date: 26 June 2013
To: Elle Reynolds
Subject: Missing you already

Darling Elle

Have arrived ok, although the flight was horrific due to turbulence. Have dealt with the notary, and everything is in order, so tomorrow I will briefly visit all three mines, which will be a nightmare with the amount of flights involved. I'm about to leave now, as all three are in the Urals, which is a fairly long way from Moscow. You would be horrified at how quickly and easily ownership is transferred in Russia, especially as Vlad had no family. There's no messing about with detailed contracts here, it's all handshakes and kickbacks. I would have loved you to have seen it, in fact, I'd love to show you Moscow, it's changed a huge amount over the years, and is a vibrant and cosmopolitan city now.
  I hope you don't work too hard while I'm away, and you allow Roger to look after you. Try not to live on toast and sandwiches. I thought we could spend a lazy weekend in Sussex, travelling down after the wake. Some quiet, peaceful time together would be lovely.
  I'm missing you like crazy.

Love you
Ivan xx

I read it a couple of times before replying.

From: Elle Reynolds
Date: 26 June 2013
To: Ivan Porenski
Subject: Missing you too

Sorry to hear about all the flights. Glad the meeting with the notary went well, although I'm surprised that companies of that value are transferred so easily. Do they not use lawyers in Russia? I would love to see Moscow one day, and visit St Basil's cathedral, built by your namesake ;)
  Please don't worry about me, I'm just working as normal, but have afternoon tea with Lady Golding booked for this afternoon, so at least I'll eat well. That only leaves tomorrow to get through, before you're home, and in my waiting arms. I'm missing you too. Please stay safe, and hurry back.

Sussex sounds like a great idea. I'd love some lazy time with you and the girls.

Love you too

Elle xxx

I pressed send, and began to work my way through the remainder of my emails. At half eight, Lewis came in. "Hi Elle, how's it going?"

I smiled. "All good. The flotation's on schedule, the factory purchase should complete next week as planned, the funds are already in our client account, and Paul Lassiter just paid his bill, so all's right with the world today."

"I heard about the non exec positions. Quite the little rising star you turned out to be. Do you think you can deliver Conde Nast?"

"I won't know too much until I attend the first board meeting, but I'll do my best. The main head office is in the states though, so I may be battling New York's finest for the work. Do you know much about our practice there? The calibre of the team?"

"I spent a bit of time seconded there a few years ago. The corporates are as sharp as knives. They'd make us look laid back and lazy. Our recruiting there is about ten times tougher than here."

"Good to know. No doubt Ivan would prefer to stick with a company he's happy with, and with me backing him up on that, we should be able to make it happen."

"Good, now I noticed you're off this afternoon. Anything nice planned?"

"Yes, for a change. I'm accompanying Lady Golding to afternoon tea, then the theatre. Taking her to see Les Miserables. Should be a nice afternoon."

"Given that she's still a shareholder in the bank, it pretty much counts as client entertainment. I'll wipe the half day off your holiday records, and turn a blind eye on your expenses form," he said, winking.

"That's kind of you, but it's social, not business, and it won't cost much. Knowing Lady Golding, she'll want to pay as it is. She likes to spend."

"Oh well, enjoy yourself, and well done for getting Lassiter to pay on time, he's notorious for making companies chase for payment." *What is it with that man and money?*

Lewis left, happy that all was well in my particular corner of his domain. Five minutes later, Laura came in bearing two cups of tea, and a notepad, to get her instructions for while I was out. As I was on top of everything, it was a short list, mainly consisting of some filing, a few things to post, and an appointment to book with Giuseppe for the day of the awards do, which to be honest, I could do myself. She looked mildly disappointed at such a short list, as she liked to be kept busy in much the same way as I did.

At two o'clock, Oscar brought Lady Golding down to my office, as she had met him for lunch at his. "Hello Elle, you look lovely dear. Is that one of the Mouret dresses? What a beautiful view you have from here."

"Nice to see you. Yes it's one of the dresses Oscar treated me to. You look lovely." She was wearing a floaty day dress, with a neat little bolero jacket, and looked extremely elegant.

"Thank you, it's a Caroline Charles design. Very cool and comfortable on such a warm day." She turned to Oscar, "thank you for a lovely lunch darling, and I'll see you at the weekend." She kissed his cheek.

"Have fun ladies," said Oscar, "mother is armed and dangerous with a credit card." He winked at me, and said his goodbyes. I shut down my computer, and led her through to the lifts.

"Such a lot of busy people. What do you all do here?" She asked, looking around the main secretaries floor.

"We do corporate law, so mergers, acquisitions, finance, flotations, that type of thing," I explained.

"What made you choose corporate as your specialism?"

"It's the most prestigious out of general law, and the most well paid really. Unless you make it to top barrister, criminal law is mostly done in prison cells, and most clients are on legal aid, and family law tends to be mostly divorces, so is quite unpleasant. Corporate is done in nice offices, and although it can be stressful, and long hours, isn't terribly harrowing. My friend Lucy does family law at our head office, and some of the cases she has to deal with can be quite distressing."

"Sounds as though you made a good choice. Your office is very nice." We travelled down in the lift. A sleek, navy blue Bentley was outside waiting for us. I slid into the air conditioned comfort, and we set off for the west end. Lady Golding told me about the places she used to frequent as a young debutante. It all sounded terribly glamorous, and exciting. "Did you ever attend a coming of age ball?" She asked.

"No, not really. I attended balls at Cambridge, which were fun, but my course was quite intense, and didn't leave as much time for socialising as other undergraduates had." I said, sidestepping the question rather neatly.

"That was a shame, still, plenty of time to make up for it now. Oscar told me how lovely you looked at that charity fundraiser a few weeks back."

"I found a super hairdresser and makeup artist in a salon near work. They were practically magicians. I just took a photo of my dress to them, and they took over. I've booked them both again for an awards dinner I've got coming up."

"I must get the number from you. I'd love a new hairstyle, but the girl who does it for me is a little set in her ways I think. I'd love to go a little blonder, and a little softer looking, more up to date." I looked at her dyed brown hair, and had to agree.

We chatted about hairstyles, handbags and perfume, as we mooched around Fortnum and Mason. Lady Golding bought herself a new bag, several pairs of shoes, and we both had a makeover in the beauty hall, purchasing new cosmetics each. She tried to pay for mine, but I refused. Oscar had already treated me, and I was happy to spend a hundred quid or so on a new look. She was delighted with hers, the makeup girl updating her frosted pink lipstick by introducing her to new, sheer pinks. By the time we were both finished, we looked great.

"I wish my daughter would do things like this," she said, as we were shown to our seats in the restaurant for our tea.

"I've not met her. Doesn't she like coming up to London?"

She sighed, "no, she's into horses and gardening. Years ago, she would have been called a blue stocking. Likes hockey, rugby and lots of fresh air. I don't think she's ever worn a scrap of makeup or a skirt in her life."

I was surprised. For all her gorgon-like qualities, Lady Golding was extremely glamorous in a dowager kind of way. "Oscar said she was in Italy. Is she studying out there?"

Lady Golding snorted. "She lives there with her 'best friend', Paulina. I don't ask questions. There are some things I'm better off not knowing. Put it this way, I think Oscar is my only hope of grandchildren, and I wasn't too sure about that a few weeks ago."

"I don't think you need to worry too much. Oscar does like women. I can vouch for that. He'll find the right one soon enough."

"I do hope so. He seems such a lonely boy at times." *Boy?*

"He seems a lot happier this last week. He came round Sunday night." We were interrupted by the waiter serving our tea. Lady Golding took a sip.

"Freshest tea in London, and the sandwiches look delicious. Yes, Oscar does seem alright. He was happy when you stayed at the castle. He seems to light up when you're around. He did tell me during our lunch today that you're seeing that Russian chap now though. He's not terribly happy about it."

"Yes, I've been seeing Ivan a couple of weeks now. I had a lecture off Oscar about it, over the terrible Conde Nast affair."

"It seemed I misjudged him over that. I thought he'd let something happen to you, so he could renege."

"He only found out at the press conference we called to publicly hand the company over to Dascha. He was genuinely very shocked. I wrote the contract giving her the company. By the way, nobody but you, Oscar and I know about this."

"I gather Oscar covered up the money trail, so please don't worry, I won't be telling anyone," she said, a steely look in her eye.

"Good, neither will I."

"I should be of the opinion that my son is the best looking man in the world, but I have to confess that I think that Russian chap is really quite something. If I was thirty years younger, you'd have a fight on your hands." We both giggled.

"My brain used to fry slightly when I first met him," I admitted, "goodness knows how I used to keep up with everything at the meetings."

"I know what you mean, even I was slightly taken aback when I first met him. Maybe I should have introduced him to my daughter. That might have tempted her."

"Probably. When I first started work there, I was told there were two men in the 'super hot club', one was Ivan, the other was Oscar. The secretaries went all useless whenever either of them turned up."

"Are the women at your office jealous because you dated both of them?"

"Not really, plus I work in an office on my own, with my own PA, so I don't have an awful lot to do with the others. Oscar's receptionist hates me though."

"I wouldn't worry about her. Oscar doesn't like that bottle blonde type. He told me she sulks whenever you've been in to see him. Silly girl should know that he would never touch the staff." She took a bite out of her smoked salmon sandwich.

"What other girls has he brought home? Does he have a type?"

She swallowed her bite, "oh yes, usually tall, slender, natural blondes, like you, but a bit taller. He's never gone for a well educated girl before though. They've usually been models or socialites. I think he liked the fact you're clever, said it was interesting and intriguing. You don't have any lawyer friends like you do you?"

"I should introduce him to my friend Lucy, she does family law. She's pretty, naturally fair, and comes from a good family. She's nice. You'd like her." In truth, I didn't know how I'd feel about Oscar being with someone else, but I couldn't keep him hanging forever, it just wasn't fair.

"And how would you feel about that?" *God, she's sharp.*

"I don't know. I have to be fair to Oscar, and encourage him to move on with his life, I am seeing Ivan now, and I doubt if Oscar would even want me, knowing I went with someone else. It's just that Oscar is so safe and dependable, which is alluring in itself. I just wish I could get over his 'quirk', but I can't."

"I'm sure the answer will reveal itself in time," she said, patting my hand. "These cakes look almost too pretty to eat don't they?" She helped herself to a tiny choux bun, and bit into it, looking ecstatic.

With tricky subjects out of the way, the rest of our tea was delightful. We sampled a couple of different types of tea, all beautifully presented in old fashioned teapots, and the cakes were out of this world.

The two of us shopped a little more after tea, perusing the womenswear department, where Lady Golding bought a couple of new day outfits, and I bought a new top, before heading over to Shaftesbury Avenue to the Queens Theatre.

Les Miserables was spellbinding, and we both loved it. Lady Golding raved about it as we walked out, and into the waiting Bentley. "Such a wonderful story, and so well produced. I'm so glad you chose it."

"I read a lot of good reviews, which is why I thought we'd both enjoy it. I'll look out for other good shows in future." We sped through to the docklands to drop me home, before Lady Golding made her way back to Sussex.

"I've had the loveliest day Elle, so thank you for arranging it, and I hope we can do it again sometime."

"Definitely. I've had a great time too." Her driver pulled up outside my flat, and I grabbed all my bags, and hopped out of the car, watching as it glided away. I had really enjoyed her company, which surprised me a little, as there was a huge generation gap as well as wildly different social positions, but I had found her to be warm, funny, and fiercely clever. Yep, I'd grown to like her.

Up in the apartment, I switched on the telly and made a coffee. It was nearly ten, but I didn't feel remotely sleepy. I checked my emails, smiling as I read a soppy one from Ivan, and replied to it equally soppily. My phone rang, I pulled it out of my bag, expecting it to be Ivan, but was pleased to see it was James.

"Hey little Elle, I got great news," he said. I smiled.

"Go on big James, what's happening?"

"I'm gonna be home early. We had a breakthrough last week, and are pretty much finished with the coding. We start testing tomorrow, and all things being well, I could be home by next Friday."

"That's fantastic news. I can't wait. I've been drooling over that holiday link you sent me. Even ordered some new bikinis and a kindle."

"I've practically lived in shorts and vests for the last two months, so it's not quite so exciting, but I'm looking forward to eating, drinking and sleeping. I've been really homesick if I'm honest. I miss the flat, London, you, and our telly programs. TV in America is rubbish."

"Well I've been spending fourteen hours a day in suits and high heels, so two weeks of flip flops and a bikini sounds like heaven to me, and I've missed you too. Sunday nights just aren't the same without you snoring on the sofa."

"I don't snore."

"I think you'll find you do. I'll record it next time for you," I teased.

"Everything alright with you?"

"Yeah, Ivan's away right now, and I have to face mum's funeral Friday, but I'm coping ok."

"Good. I'll cook us both a huge roast when I get back. I've been dreaming about it for weeks."

"Mmm, I do miss your roasts. I feel like I've lived on ready meals and sandwiches for months."

"Naughty girl. You're too thin as it is. Anyway, I'd better go get on with some work. I'll call you next week when I know a firm time yeah?"

"Great. See you soon." We said our goodbyes, and I headed off to bed.

Chapter 16

The following day seemed to drag on forever. My work was tedious, and rather mundane contract stuff, which required intense concentration, mainly because it was so boring, and monotonous. The office itself seemed a little quiet, as we were in holiday season, and people had begun to take their leave. Most companies put merger plans on hold through July and August, so with the exception of a few other projects, there wasn't much else to do. I left at six, nipping down to the arcade to buy some food at the deli, some milk, and a few pairs of new stockings. I walked back to the flat, and was just about to put my code in the pad to open the door to the lobby, when a woman approached me.

"Excuse me, do you live here?"

"Yes, why?" I looked closely at her. She was small and pretty, with fair hair, piercing blue eyes, and a deep, golden tan. She didn't look like a nutter.

"I'm looking for a James Harrison, he used to live in the penthouse. Do you know if he's moved?"

"I'm his flatmate, Elle, and no he hasn't moved, but he's away working in the states at the moment. I can give him a message for you."

"Would you mind? I did write to him a few weeks ago, and didn't hear from him, and that explains why." She got a pen and piece of paper out of her handbag, and scribbled down a phone number. "Can you tell him that Janine needs to speak to him, and it's rather urgent please." I stared at her, wondering if she was his ex.

"Sure, I'll pass it on." I took the number from her, and watched as she wandered away, before tapping in my code, and heading in. I called James straight away, and gave him the message, and the phone number. He seemed stunned, asking what she looked like. I described her. He confirmed that it was indeed his ex, and he would give her a call to find out what she wanted.

With my good deed for the day done, I heated up my ready meal, and made a latte, before checking my outfit for the funeral, and finally sinking into a deep bath. I was dreading facing the final reality of mum's death, but would be relieved to see Ivan safely home.

Next morning, I hit the gym at my usual time, using a punishing workout to relieve some of the tension I felt at facing the day. I got back to the flat by eight, and pottered around, before dressing in my black Mouret dress, with black stockings and black Jimmy Choos, putting them on like a suit of armour. With my black Prada bag at the ready, all I had to do was wait for Ivan. I made a coffee, and sat playing with my phone. When it rang, I nearly dropped the damn thing. I answered, and it was Roger, telling me that Ivan's plane had been delayed, and I should go on ahead without him. Less than five minutes later, Roger buzzed me to tell me he was downstairs. I grabbed my things, and headed down.

In the car, I got the distinct feeling that something was 'off'. "Ivan is alright, isn't he?" I asked.

"Yes, of course, his flight was delayed, and he's currently in the air. He sends his apologies."

I wanted to scream LIAR at him, and a pernicious, prickling fear crept over my body. I knew full well that Roger wouldn't tell me the truth if he'd been instructed to lie, so all I could do was wait. I tried to call Ivan, but his phone went straight to voicemail.

I watched Roger carefully as we drove to Welling. He was giving nothing away, his face was an impenetrable mask. We pulled up outside the flat, and I left Roger in the car, and rang the bell of Mum's old flat. Ray answered looking dishevelled, and invited me in. The flat looked like Beirut, with pizza boxes and mouldy coffee cups laying around, and a collection of empty beer cans growing in a corner. "Let me brush my teeth, and I'm ready. Would you make us a cuppa while you wait?" He mumbled, "only

I got a bit wankered down at the Green man last night, so until I can get another beer, my mouth feels like dust."

"You're going to my mum's funeral with a hangover? What the fuck is the matter with you? At least have a shave and a shower for fucks sake. Show some sodding respect." I felt ashamed at falling back down to his level, and swearing at him, but it was the only language he understood. He shuffled off into the bathroom, and I went to see if I could make a cup of tea.

For a start, the milk was so off, it was practically cheese, so I sent Roger down to the corner shop for milk, tea bags, and some washing up liquid and sponges. When he came back, I washed up two cups, and made a drink. I looked around the wreck of my old home, marvelling at how quickly it had got into such a terrible state. When Ray appeared, he at least looked a little cleaner, and had put on his least dirty shirt. He explained that he didn't have a black tie to wear, and hadn't wanted to waste benefit money on something that he'd only wear once. *Loser.*

At half eleven, the hearses arrived, with the arrangement of lilies I'd ordered, the only flowers present. My heart broke again for her. I was glad that I'd bought a nice big arrangement to decorate her coffin, as no other bastard had bothered. The neighbours began to come out of their houses to line the street, which I found strangely comforting. Ray and I climbed in the only car, and set off behind the hearse. Roger allowed mum's downstairs neighbours to hitch a lift in the Mercedes while he followed behind me. The rest of the cortège was made up of old Fords and some rusty Fiats, as we slowly made our way out of Lovell Avenue for the last time.

The crematorium at Eltham was a lovely place, with pretty gardens of remembrance, and plenty of tranquil spaces for reflection. The undertakers lifted Mum's coffin in, and I was struck by how tiny it looked, and how effortlessly they carried it. They placed it on a plinth in front of a pair of curtains, and retreated as we all filed in to the strains of 'Bridge over troubled water', her favourite song.

I couldn't tell you much about the service, or the reading, as I felt as though I was in a dream world. It was the most surreal experience of my life, saying the final goodbye to the woman who had tried so hard for me, and who had sacrificed so much to help me escape the life she had endured. She hadn't had dreams of her own, but she'd helped me with mine, even when she hadn't understood them, or even agreed with them. My tears began to fall. A tissue appeared by my shoulder, held out by a neighbour who was sitting in the row behind. I took it gratefully, and dabbed my eyes. At the end of the service, the curtains opened, and the coffin slid away. I said a silent goodbye, before standing to leave.

It was then that I noticed that the chapel was packed. Friends and neighbours had all turned out to pay their respects, and say their goodbyes to a woman who had been a good friend, and a popular person in the street. I managed a wan smile, and nodded at a few of the people who had been close friends of hers, and headed back to the car.

The landlord of the pub did us proud. He had laid on a lovely spread, and roped off part of the lounge bar for our exclusive use. We packed the place out, and once the initial scrum at the bar was dealt with, it all went very smoothly. I moved around the room, thanking people for coming, and listening to their stories about mum. It was nice, hearing how popular she was, and how well liked she'd been. If she'd been there, she would have loved it.

I stayed for at least two hours, before saying my goodbyes, and leaving them to it. Ray was taking advantage of all the sympathetic free drinks he was being bought, and I really didn't want to be lumbered with getting him home.

I slid into the Mercedes, and asked Roger to take me home. "Did everything go alright?" He asked. I didn't answer, as I was looking at forty two missed calls on my mobile, all from various numbers. "Elle, I said was everything alright?" Roger asked again.

"Before I call all these numbers, perhaps you can tell me?"

He sighed, "I was under strict instructions that you shouldn't be told until your mother's funeral was over. Ivan and his guards went missing last night just before they were about to take off. They were intercepted before they got on the plane. It's being reported on the news now." I quickly scrolled through my iPhone to sky news, and read that Ivan's group had been overpowered and kidnapped just before getting on his private jet to leave Russia, and it was believed they were being held hostage somewhere in the Urals mountains. I went cold, and felt sick.

Shaking, I worked my way through the missed calls, speaking to Ms Pearson, Mr Ranenkiov, Lewis and finally Oscar.

"Is there anything you can do? Any contacts that could help?" I asked, after sliding up the privacy screen in the car.

"Until there's a demand, not a huge amount, but I know someone who can, and he owes you."

"Who?"

"Darius. Works for the intelligence services. He'll know what to do. I may get him to call you. If you need ransom money, Elle, you can come to me."

"Thank you. I'm on my way to my company head office to see Ms Pearson. She called to say she needed to see me immediately."

"Keep your phone switched on, and answer all calls straightaway."

"Will do."

We were driving over London Bridge when Darius called. "Elle, Oscar contacted me. It seems you need some assistance?"

"Yes, I take it you know about Ivan going missing?"

"Yes, we've already had some contact with the KGB over the matter. The good news is that he is still alive."

"But?"

"A ransom demand has been given to the Russian equivalent of our foreign secretary. They want fifty million dollars."

"Oscar said he would pay it. I'm sure Ivan will pay it back. So how do we do this?"

"I need to make some calls, it's not as simple as just paying the ransom. The Russian government can't be seen to capitulate to hostage demands, so we have to be sneaky. Usually what happens is that the money is paid, and the hostage released alongside the illusion of a rescue attempt which is triumphant. That way, nobody loses face."

"How long will it take?"

"I don't know. Our diplomats are with the Russian government at the moment, working on this. I'll speak to Oscar about a secret money transfer, and we'll do our best to get him out as fast as we can. I do know that I owe you, you know."

"Darius, please do this for me because I'm a nice girl, in love with a man who's been kidnapped, not because of an imaginary debt. I gave you both my word, and it will stand until I die."

"Ivan is one lucky man to have you. I'll do my very best to get him out alive, and twist every arm that I can." We said our goodbyes, and he promised to call as soon as he had updates. Shortly afterwards, we pulled up at the Pearson Hardwick head office. I was immediately whisked up to Ms Pearson's office, and shown straight in. We shook hands, and sat down.

"So, how are you bearing up? And have you heard any news yet?"

"There's been a ransom demand made. People are trying their best to get him out alive, but I don't know yet if it will happen, or when."

Ms Pearson looked grave. "As you possibly know, I met with Mr Porenski to put in place plans should this scenario happen. As of now, you are acting as managing director of all his companies. We're you aware of that plan being in place?"

"Yes I was, although I did suggest I didn't have the experience or knowledge to do it."

"Just caretake it. Don't let the other directors make any important decisions. Aim for keeping things on an even a keel as you can, given the circumstances. You're a clever woman Elle, and Ivan knows you can be trusted more than any man in his company. There's one more thing he asked me to alert you of in a scenario such as this."

I looked Ms Pearson in the eye. "First I need to ask, what do I do if he doesn't come back?"

She paused. "You get on with running your companies, because he left everything to you. That's what he asked me to tell you."

ABOUT THE AUTHOR

D A Latham is a salon owner, mother of Persian cats, a dog called Ted, and devoted partner to the wonderful Allan.

Other books by D A Latham

The Beauty and the Blonde

A very Corporate Affair Book 1

A very Corporate affair book 3

The Taming of the Oligarch

Printed in Great Britain
by Amazon